簡明初級英文法

英文法

上

謝國平　編著

三民書局

國家圖書館出版品預行編目資料

簡明初級英文法／謝國平編著.－－初版十二刷.－
－臺北市：三民，2009
　　冊；　　公分
ISBN 978–957–14–1931–2　（上冊）
ISBN 978–957–14–1932–9　（下冊）

1.英國語言—文法

805.16/8255　　V.2

© 　**簡明初級英文法（上）**

編著者	謝國平
發行人	劉振強
著作財產權人	三民書局股份有限公司 臺北市復興北路386號
發行所	三民書局股份有限公司 地址／臺北市復興北路386號 電話／(02)25006600 郵撥／0009998–5
印刷所	三民書局股份有限公司
門市部	復北店／臺北市復興北路386號 重南店／臺北市重慶南路一段61號

初版一刷　1992年9月
初版十二刷　2009年6月
編　　號　S 800820
行政院新聞局登記證局版臺業字第○二○○號

ISBN　978–957–14–1931–2　（上冊：平裝）
http://www.sanmin.com.tw　三民網路書店

序

　　國民中學的英語教材近年來以溝通教學法為編寫的基礎。在可見的未來時日裏，注重溝通的教學法將是國中英語教材的骨幹。雖然溝通教學法特別注重語意及語用的功能，但是，語意及語用是建構於文法的基礎上。如果文法不對，即使能溝通，充其量其英語只是洋涇濱英語。因此，雖然現行國中教科書上沒有「文法」這一欄，但其句型部分卻也是文法結構的介紹。

　　然而，編者總認為，在學習英語初期雖然不必刻意強調文法教學，但基本的結構體認還是必需的。對文法的認識也應該循序且有系統地培養。基於這種理念，編者決定以《簡明現代英文法》為基礎，選取適合國中程度的內容，精簡成一本國中學生適用的文法書，希望能配合國中的英語課本，增強學生對英語文法結構的了解，作為進一步培養聽、說、讀、寫四技能的基礎。

　　本書編寫的原則，與《簡明現代英文法》無異——文字要簡易，資料要新，語用原理原則要說明，習題要足夠。然而要達成此四原則並使內容切合國中學生的程度與需要，實非易事。編寫過程中，雖盡力以過去多年輔導中學英語教學經驗作為取材及設計習題的參考，但疏漏及不週延之處定難全免。尚祈使用本書的教師、學生以及所有讀者多予指正，是所至感。

謝國平　謹誌

臺北　師大英語系

八十一年五月

主要參考資料

Aronson, Trudy. *English Grammar Digest*. Englewood Cliffs, New Jersey: Prentice-Hall, Inc., 1984.

Jesperson, Otto. *A Modern English Grammar: On Historical Principle*. Vol.1 – Vol.7.

Marcellar, Frank. *Modern English: A Pratical Reference Guide*. Englewood Cliffs, New Jersey: Prentice-Hall, Inc., 1972.

Murphy, Raymond. *English Grammar in Use*. London: Cambridge University Press, 1985.

Quirk, Randolph, Sidney Greenbaum, Geoffrey Leech, and Jan Svartvik. *A Grammar of Contemporary English*. London: Longman, 1972.

Quirk, Randolph, Sidney Greenbaum, Geoffrey Leech, and Jan Svartvik. *A Comprehensive Grammar of the English Language*. London: Longman, 1985.

Swan, Michael. *Practical English Usage*. Oxford: Oxford University Press, 1980.

Swan, Michael. *Basic English Usage*. Oxford: Oxford University Press, 1984.

Thompson, A. J., & A. V. Martinet. *A Practical English Grammar*. 4 th edition, Hong Kong: Oxford University Press, 1986.

Wren, P. C. and H. Martin. *High School English Composition*. Bombay: K. & J. Cooper, 1962.

《簡明現代英文法》

簡明初級英文法(上)
目次

序

主要參考資料

第一章　認識英語文

第二章　英語文法的結構單位

第三章　詞類與文法功能

第四章　句型略要

第五章　動詞的種類與形式

第六章　動詞的時式

第七章　被動語態

第八章　主要助動詞 Be、Have、Do

第九章　情態助動詞

第十章　問句的形成

第十一章　否定句的形成

第十二章　名詞

第十三章　代名詞

第十四章　主詞與動詞的一致

第一章
認識英語文

　　我們寫這本書的目的只有一個, 就是要以簡易的方式把英語文法介紹給初學英語的學生, 使他們能明瞭英語文法基本結構, 因而對學習英語有助。

　　但是, 在正式談及英語文法之前, 我們要對英語本身有所認識。當然, 有關英語, 可談的課題很多, 但對初階的國中學生而言, 我們至少應該知道英語與英文的分別、英語文的重要性、以及什麼是英語文法。

1.1. 英語與英文

　　⑴在一般人看來, 英語跟英文是不分的, 都指 English 一字。但事實上, 語與文是有分別的。簡單地說, **發聲而說出來的是英語, 以文字寫下來的是英文。**

　　英文要比英語在體裁上比較正式, 對文法及用字的要求也比較嚴格。例如在口語中常常可以省略一些語詞:

　　　　"Seen Mary lately?" 「最近見過 Mary 沒有?」

　　　　"No." 「沒有。」

但在書面的英文裏, 上面第一句就要寫成 Have you seen Mary lately?

　　從這例子看來, 英語與英文是有所分別的, 但是無論英語或英文, 都有

它的法則。也就是說，英語雖然比較不正式，但也不能違反文法規則。比方說，如果我們把上面的"Seen Mary lately?"說成"Lately Mary seen?"❶就不合文法，使別人聽了之後覺得不對勁了。

　　因此，我們應該知道，英語和英文在體裁、用字等方面會有差異，但是，大多數的文法規則對英語及英文都適用。因爲「英語」一詞的語義比較廣，我們在這本書中採用「英語」來泛指英語與英文。

　　(2)英語是一種分佈區域很廣的語言。現代英語如以地區來分，有英式英語、美式英語、蘇格蘭英語、愛爾蘭英語、加拿大英語、南非英語、澳洲英語、紐西蘭英語等。這些地區大多數以英語爲第一語言或母語來使用，雖然其中每一種英語都有差異，但是文法還是絕大部分相同的。一般文法書所描述的所謂標準英語文法，都是指這相同的部分，特別是以英式及美式英語爲準則。我們在這本書中，也採用這種廣義的標準，但是會稍微偏重美式英語。不過，如果遇到英式英語與美式英語有明顯的差異時，我們也會盡量指出來。

1.2.　英語的重要

　　今天，我們每個中學生都在學英語，但是，對大多數人而言，英語只是一種學科，是學校裏必須唸的一種課程。很多人都不知道爲什麼要學英語。事實上，在那麼多種外語中，我們整個社會以及教育系統，特別重視英語，並非毫無理由的。最顯然而重要的理由是，英語比其他外語來得重要。

　　就每個人來說，英語無論在學校的學業或在社會中的事業上都是無比重

---

❶我們採用一般語言學書中常用的方式，對於有問題或不大妥當或不合文法的句子，在前面用星號*標示。

要的。在學校裏是主科之一，在工作上是有利的工具之一。從社會及國家的層面看，英語的重要性更是明顯。英語是現今國際貿易使用最廣的語言，英語是國際航空的共同語、英語更是資訊及科技的最主要語言，全世界的廣播大約有百分之六十使用英語，全球的郵件大約有百分之七十用英語書寫。❷國際文獻協會(FID, Federation Internationale de Documentation)在八十年代前幾年曾指出，在全世界龐大的科技文獻中，大約有百分之八十五的資訊是用英語儲存下來的。因此，要使用這些資訊，也是非透過英語不可。❸由此看來，我們個人在學業或事業上，整個國家在經貿與科技的發展上，英語都是不可或缺的工具。

1.3.　英語文法

我們都知道，說話及寫作時都須遵守一定的規則，例如在語詞的順序、字形的變化等都有一定的規則，不能任意的說或寫。否則，我們說出來或寫出來的話就會被認爲不通，不對，或是更常說的，不合文法。因此，最廣義的說法是，文法就是某一語言說話及寫作的法則。英語文法就是使用英語時，說及寫的法則。

一般英語文法書多以詞類與句子結構爲重點，本書也不例外。在以下各章裏，我們將分別討論各種語詞、詞組、句子的結構及用法。

---

❷參看 Quirk 等(1972), *A Grammar of Contemporary English*, 1.20, p.17.

❸參看謝國平(1984), 〈英語教學與科技發展〉, 刊於《明日的科學教育》, 臺北: 幼獅出版社, pp.445-453.

《**習題 1**》

1.略述英語與英文的分別。

2.略述英語的重要性。

第二章
英語文法的結構單位

　　英語的**句子**由**詞組**(片語或子句)組成，詞組由**單字**(word)組成，單字由**字根**(root)單獨構成，或由字根加上**附加成分**(affix)而組成；當然，所有的字根及附加成分都由**語音**所組成。因此，在認識英語文法時，我們必須認識英語這些基本的結構單位。

2.1.　英語的語音

　　英語的書寫符號(字母)只有 26 個，但語音却不只 26 個。以 K.K.音標來表示，英語的語音列舉如下：

母音：i, ɪ, ɛ, æ, a, ɑ, ɔ, u, ʊ, ʌ, ɝ, ɚ, ə, e, o, aɪ, aʊ, ɔɪ(K.K.所描述的是一般的美國發音，我們所列舉的只是這種發音中最基本的語音，因此數目並不是絕對的，如把與 r 結合的母音也計算在內，或將一些地方方音也列出的話，母音數目會更多一些。)

子音：p, b, t, d, k, g, f, v, θ, ð, s, z, ʃ, ʒ, h, tʃ, dʒ, m, n, ŋ, m̩, n̩, l, l̩, w, hw, j, r

　　這四十幾個語音都由 26 個字母拼寫，因此經常會有同一字母代表不同的語音，以及同一語音可以用不同字母或字母群來表示的情形，使學生產生學習上的困擾。但近年來國中教科書中所介紹的 phonics 教學法(介紹語音與拼寫法之規律關係)多少對學習有所幫助。本書並非英語語音學的書，因此我們不在這裏介紹發音與拼字的細節。在這一節中，我們只是指出，構成英語單字的語音有四十幾個，書寫英文的字母只有 26 個。

2.2.　字根

　　字根(又叫做詞根)是**不含任何附加成分**(如字首或字尾)的單字。例如：
　　　　boy、girl、book、walk、play 等
但是 boys、girls、player、walking 等就不算是字根了，因為這幾個字中，每個都多加了一個附加成分，字尾-s、-er、或-ing。

2.3.　附加成分(Affixes)

　　英語在構詞時，附加成分**只用「字首」**(prefix)**和「字尾」**(suffix)兩種。
常用的字首如：
　　　表示否定的：un-、non-、in-、dis-等
　　　表示輕蔑或貶抑的：mis-、mal-、pseudo-等
　　　表示程度或大小的：arch-、super-、sub-、over-、mini-等
　　　表示態度的：co-、anti-、pro-等
　　　表示地方或處所的：intra-、inter-、trans-、sub-等
　　　表示時間或順序的：fore-、post-、pre-、ex-等

常用的字尾如：

-s、-ed、-ing、-er、-ful、-y、-ly、-(i)an、-ese、-ist、-tion、
-ation、-ism、-ify、-ity、-en、-less、-ive、-ic、-ish、-able 等

2.4.　字

凡是可以單獨使用而含有意思的語音組合，都可以稱爲「字」或「單字」
(word)。因此，boy、girl、boys、girls、play、player、players、store、
walk 等，都是英語的字。字首或字尾如-s、-tion、-ly、non-、mis-、in-、
sub-等，因爲不能單獨使用，因此不能算字。我們可以說

　　I am a student. 我是一個學生。
但却不能說
　　*I am a -ful.
或　　*She is a dis-.
因爲-ful 與 dis-都不能單獨使用，因此也不能算是一個字。
　　字在英語文法裏非常重要，因爲所有的句子都是以字爲基礎而構成的。

2.5.　片語

「片語」簡單地說就是一群單字的組合。當然，我們知道，不是隨意地把
幾個單字湊合在一起就可以稱爲片語(phrase)的。在形式上會有一些特徵，
如由介詞引導的叫做「介詞片語」(preposition phrase)，含不定詞的叫做
「不定詞片語」(infinitive　phrase)，含分詞的叫做「分詞片語」(participle
phrase)。在文法功能上，片語可以當名詞、形容詞、或副詞使用，所以我

們也有「**名詞片語**」(noun phrase)、「**形容詞片語**」(adjective phrase)、「**副詞片語**」(adverb phrase)等名稱。以下例句中，斜體部分都是片語：

1. The boy is standing *by the chair.*　那個男孩子站在椅子旁。
2. *To work hard* is very important.　勤勉地工作是很重要的事。
3. The girl *standing by the window* is my sister.　站在窗子旁邊的女孩子是我的姊姊。

上面第一例句中的 by the chair 在形式上是介詞片語，功能上是副詞片語，修飾動詞 is standing；第二句中的 To work hard 形式上是不定詞片語，功能上是名詞片語，做句子的主詞；第三句中的 standing by the window 形式上是分詞片語，功能上是形容詞片語，修飾名詞 The girl。事實上，第三句的主詞 The girl standing by the window 也可稱作名詞片語，因為它的功能等於名詞，做這例句的主詞。

2.6.　子句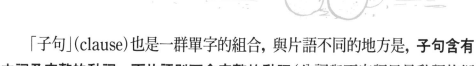

「子句」(clause)也是一群單字的組合，與片語不同的地方是，**子句含有主詞及完整的動詞，而片語則不含完整的動詞**(分詞與不定詞只是動詞的衍生形式，本身不作句子的動詞使用)。

子句常含有一個從屬連接詞或關係代名詞，作為引導子句的字。子句通常有三種：

1. **名詞子句**(noun clause)：
   I know *that he lives there.*　我知道他住在那兒。
2. **形容詞子句**(adjective clause)：

The boy *who is speaking to Mary* enjoys playing soccer.
正在跟 Mary 說話的那個男孩子喜歡踢足球。

3. 副詞子句(adverb clause):

He did not come to school *because he was sick yesterday.*
他昨天因為生病而沒有來上課。

以上三個斜體印刷的子句分別含有引導詞 that、 who、及 because;
that 引導的子句作動詞 know 的受詞, who 引導的子句修飾 boy, because
引導的子句修飾主句動詞 did not come。

2.7. 句子

傳統文法通常以語意或功能來給「句子」(sentence)下定義。因此, 很多
文法書會說, 句子是能表達一個完整語意的字群, 有些書則說, 句子是包括
一個「主詞」(subject)及一個「述語」(predicate)的組合。主詞常是句子所要
談論的主題, 而述語則是用來闡述這主題的部分。

如果我們把這兩種看法加起來, 也可以說, **句子是敘述一個完整語意的**
字群, 在結構上包含一個主詞及一個述語, 而述語中含有一個完整的動詞。

在英文的書面語中, 句子第一個單字要以大寫字母開始, 最後一個單字
後面要加句號(.), 或問號(?), 或感嘆號(!)。

以下各例都是英語的句子:

The child ate his apple. (陳述句, statement)這小孩子吃了他
的蘋果。

Did he eat his apple? (問句, question)他吃了他的蘋果嗎?

Stand up. (祈使句, imperative)站起來。

How beautiful she is! (感嘆句, exclamation)她多美啊!

What a pity!　(感嘆句, exclamation)眞可惜!

《習題 2》

(A)試寫出下列各單字的字根部分。

　　例: boys

　　　　字根: *boy*

1. careful

2. quickly

3. books

4. dangerous

5. loudly

6. freed

7. player

8. parents

9. jogging

(B)試指出下列單字中的字首及字尾, 以 p 表示字首, s 表示字尾。

　　例: play*er* (s)

　　　　*un*happy (p)

1. drinking

2. bigger

3. thinker

4. suddenly

5. disagree

6. subset

7. unimportant

8. thinner

9. comfortable

10. frankly

(C)試指出下列各句中的片語。

　例：The book is *on the table.*

1. He swims every day.

2. She left in a hurry.

3. Alice is learning English for fun.

4. English is spoken all over the world.

5. She wanted to come here early.

6. Let us bring the cow into the barn.

(D)試指出下列各句子中的從屬子句。

　例：I saw the book *that she bought yesterday.*

1. We know that Mr. Lin is John's uncle.

2. A person who teaches English is an English teacher.

3. It is not easy to run fast when you become old.

4. Though he is rich, he is not happy.

5. I like Mary because she is honest.

6. If you come here tomorrow, you will see our new history teacher.

第三章
詞類與文法功能

3.1. 詞類（Parts of Speech）

　　從上面一章我們知道，句子由單字組成。單字按照文法上的特性，又可分為幾種不同的種類，我們稱之為「詞類」。

　　英語中常見的詞類大致分為以下幾種：**名詞**(noun)、**代名詞**(pronoun)、**動詞**(verb)、**形容詞**(adjective)、**副詞**(adverb)、**介系詞**(常簡稱為介詞, preposition)、**連接詞**(conjunction)、以及**感嘆詞**(interjection)。此外，**冠詞**(article)在英語的地位相當重要，所以很多文法書都會以特別的章節來討論。

⑴名詞（Noun）

　　名詞是人、地、事、物或概念的名稱。例如：Tom、Taipei、table、key、love、honesty 等。

　　名詞可分為：「專有名詞」、「普通名詞」、「抽象名詞」、「物質名詞」、「集合名詞」等。

　　1.「**專有名詞**」(proper noun)是特定的人、地、事物的名稱, 拼寫時要

以**大寫字母起首**。例如: Peter、Tom、Alice、Mary、Taipei、New York、London、Sunday、October、Christmas 等。

　　2.「**普通名詞**」(common noun)是一般, 而非特定的人、地、事物共同的名稱, 拼寫時不必以大寫開始。例如: boy、girl、man、dog、city、table、chair、apple、box、hat 等。

　　3.「**物質名詞**」(mass noun 或稱 material noun)指構成物體的不可分的質與材料等。例如: water、air、coffee、iron、wool、paper、milk、bread 等。

　　4.「**抽象名詞**」(abstract noun)為事物的性質、特性以及抽象的想法、概念等的名稱。例如: love(愛)、beauty(美)、courage(勇氣)、happiness (幸福)、honesty(誠實)等。

　　5.「**集合名詞**」(collective noun)為一群人、動物或事物整體的名稱。例如: crowd(群眾)、team(隊)、class(班)、committee(委員會)、herd(群)、party(政黨)、family(家庭)等。

　　以上的分類, 也可以用字尾可不可以加上表示複數的詞尾-s 來分為「可數名詞」與「不可數名詞」。**普通及集合名詞是可數名詞, 而抽象、專有、及物質名詞是不可數名詞。**

　　以下各例句中, 斜體的語詞為名詞:

1. *John* bought two *books* yesterday.　John 昨天買了兩本書。
2. He doesn't like *milk*.　他不喜歡牛奶。
3. *Tom* doesn't have any *respect* for Mary.　Tom 對 Mary 一點也不尊敬。
4. My *family* are all well.　我的家人都很健康。

⑵代名詞(Pronoun)

用來代替名詞的字稱為「代名詞」。代名詞可以分為「人稱代名詞」、「指

示代名詞」、「疑問代名詞」、「不定代名詞」、以及「關係代名詞」等幾大類。

1. **人稱代名詞**(personal pronoun)有：

I, me　我　　　　　　　　we, us　我們

you, you　你　　　　　　 you, you　你們

he, him　他　　　　　　　they, them　他(她、它)們

she, her　她

it, it　它

2. **指示代名詞**(demonstrative pronoun)有：

this　這　　　　　　　　these　這些

that　那　　　　　　　　those　那些

3. **疑問代名詞**(interrogative pronoun)有：

who, whom　誰

whose　誰的

which　哪個、哪些

what　什麼

4. **不定代名詞**(indefinite pronoun)常用的有：

all　所有的人或事物　　　each　每一個

both　兩者　　　　　　　everybody　每一個人

everyone　每一個人　　　many　多數(人或物)

few　少數(人或物)　　　none　無人(物)

neither　兩者都不　　　　no one　無人

nobody　無人　　　　　　several　幾個(人或物)

one　一個(人或物)　　　someone　某人

some　一些(人或物)　　　any　任何的人或事物

somebody　某人　　　　　anyone　任何人

either　兩者中任一個　　　anybody　任何人

　　5.關係代名詞(relative pronoun)用來引導一個形容詞子句，它們包括：

who, whom, whose, which, what, that

以下例句中，斜體的語詞為代名詞。

　　1. *He* gave *me* ten dollars.　他給我十塊錢。(人稱代名詞)

　　2. Tom doesn't like *these*.　Tom 不喜歡這些。(指示代名詞)

　　3. *What* did Alice want?　Alice 想要什麼？(疑問代名詞)

　　4. *Everybody* likes Mary.　每個人都喜歡 Mary。(不定代名詞)

　　5. The girl *who* is standing by the window is Tom's sister.
　　　站在窗子旁邊的女孩子是 Tom 的姊姊。(關係代名詞)

⑶動詞（Verb）

　　表示動作或狀態的語詞稱為動詞。動詞分為「**普通動詞**」及「**助動詞**」兩大類，普通動詞為動詞的核心，助動詞通常與普通動詞連用，形成完整的動詞組。

　　以下各句中，斜體的語詞為動詞，或助動詞＋動詞的動詞組合：

　　1. Tom *hit* John.　Tom 打了 John。

　　2. He *drank* some milk.　他喝了一些牛奶。

　　3. Our teacher *looked* very tired.　我們的老師看起來很疲倦。

　　4. He *ran* away.　他跑開了。

　　5. She *is* ill.　她生病了。

　　6. We *can swim.*　我們會游泳。

　　7. He *has done* his homework.　他已經做完功課了。

　　8. I *will see* him tomorrow.　我明天會見他。

⑷形容詞（Adjective）

用來修飾名詞或代名詞的語詞稱爲形容詞，例如：

blue eyes　藍眼睛　　　　*large* city　大城市

fat man　胖子　　　　　*ten* apples　十個蘋果

cold season　寒冷的季節　　*this* student　這個學生

形容詞告訴我們有關名詞的種類、特性、數目等訊息。

⑸副詞（Adverb）

修飾動詞、形容詞，或另一副詞的語詞稱爲副詞。副詞常提供有關動作或性質的「狀態」、「時間」、「地點」、「程度」等的訊息。例如：

1. She is singing *loudly*.　她正在大聲歌唱。（狀態）
2. He told her the news *immediately*.　他立刻把消息告訴她。（時間）
3. I went *there*.　我到那兒去。（地方）
4. She is *very* clever.　她很聰明。（程度）

⑹介系詞（Preposition）

介系詞置於名詞或代名詞前面，表示這名詞或代名詞與句子中其他某些語詞之間的關係。介系詞常簡稱爲「**介詞**」，有些文法書稱之爲「**前置詞**」。介詞後面的名詞或代名詞爲介詞的受詞，代名詞要用受格形式。例如：

1. We will see you *after* dinner.　我們晚飯之後會見你。
2. The book is *on* the desk.　書在桌子上。
3. I bought the book *for* her.　我買這本書給她。
4. Everyone *in* the room laughed loudly.　房間裏的每個人都大聲地笑。

常用的介詞有:

about	after	along	at
before	behind	below	by
down	for	from	in
into	of	on	over
to	under	until	up
upon	with 等		

(7)連接詞 (Conjunction)

用來連接單字、片語、子句之語詞稱爲連接詞。例如:

1. Tom *and* Jack are here.　Tom 和 Jack 都來了。(連接兩個單字 [名詞])

2. Did he go there by bus *or* by taxi?　他是坐公共汽車或是坐計程車到那兒的呢?　(連接兩個片語 [介詞片語])

3. Your teacher came here yesterday *and* he looked very happy.　你的老師昨天到這兒來, 他看起來很愉快。(連接兩個子句)

4. I will wait *until* you come here.　我會一直等到你來這兒。(連接兩個子句)

連接詞通常分爲「**對等連接詞**」及「**從屬連接詞**」兩種。常用的對等連接詞有:

　　and、or、but、for、nor

常用的從屬連接詞有:

　　after、because、before、how、if、that、than、until、when、where 等

(8)感嘆詞(Interjection)

感嘆詞表示情緒，與句子中其他語詞並無文法上的關係。例如：

My goodness! What have you done?　我的天啊！你做了什麼？

Oh, what a beautiful girl she is!　啊，她是個多麼美麗的女孩呀！

Bravo!　好極了！

Ouch!　哎唷！

(9)冠詞(Article)

冠詞分爲「**定冠詞**」(definite article)及「**不定冠詞**」(indefinite article)兩種。定冠詞爲 *the*，不定冠詞爲 *a* 及 *an*。冠詞置於名詞前面，爲名詞指標的一種。冠詞主要的功能是指出跟隨在它後面的名詞是有所特指或是不定的人或事物。例如：

I want to buy *a* radio.　我想買一部收音機。

The man in *the* car is my uncle.　在那輛車子裏的人是我的叔叔。

《習題 3》

(A)請將下面各句中的名詞選出，並註明其種類。

例：*John* is a student.(專有名詞)

He is a *boy*.(普通名詞)

1. He likes English.
2. The house belongs to Mr. Smith.

3. The man bought a house.

4. His wife sells typewriters.

5. My family are all well.

6. No one can live without water.

7. I bought some milk at the supermarket.

8. The committee have nothing to say.

(B)請在下列各句中，選出代名詞。

1. She is sitting by the window.

2. We are looking at the picture.

3. Mary likes the dress which she bought yesterday.

4. Anyone can answer this question.

5. If you come early, you can certainly see Janet.

6. What did he want?

7. I cannot understand the question. It is too difficult.

(C)請將下列句子中的動詞或動詞組(助動詞＋動詞)選出。

1. The children were playing in the garden.

2. We saw Tom yesterday.

3. Bees gather honey from flowers.

4. He has finished reading the book.

5. Tom ran downstairs.

6. Do you know Mr. Johnson?

7. Will you come tomorrow?

8. She looked very happy.

(D)在下列各句中請將形容詞及副詞選出，分別註明，並以箭號指出被修飾之語詞。

例：The *tall* boy ran *fast.*

　　　tall(形容詞)　　fast(副詞)

1. He gave us the correct answer very quickly.

2. Mary is very clever.

3. Although Mr. Smith is blind, he is a skillful mechanic.

4. The students walked very slowly.

5. You must go now.

6. If it rains, we will not go on a picnic tomorrow.

(E)將下列各句中的介詞及連接詞選出，並分別註明。

　例：The book is *on* the desk.(介系詞)

　　　John came in *and* sat down quietly.(連接詞)

1. John is tall but Mary is short.

2. If you come here tomorrow, you will see Tom.

3. Toys and books are all over the floor.

4. Please wait for me.

5. Please don't stand by the window.

6. Everyone in class was happy and excited.

7. When he came into the classroom, he saw Larry sitting at his desk.

3.2.　文法功能

　　從上面第二章 2.7.節中，我們知道英語的句子分爲主詞及述語兩部分。「主詞」爲句子所要談論的主題，「述語」用來闡述這主題。

　　句子中每一個字都屬於某種詞類，但是也同時具有固定的文法功能。大體上，英語的句子裏，除了動詞作述語的核心以外，主要的文法功能有三種：

「**主詞**」(subject)、「**受詞**」(object)、及「**修飾語**」(modifier)。

(1)主詞

　　「**主詞**」是述語中動詞的「主事者」，如動詞爲表示動作的動詞，主詞就是做這動作的人或動物。如動詞表示狀態或情況，主詞就是處於這種情況或狀態的人或事物。主詞由名詞、代名詞、或具名詞功用的「名詞相等語」(noun equivalent)表示。以下例句中，斜體的字爲主詞：

1. *Tom* saw Mary.　　Tom 看見 Mary。(名詞)
2. *He* is happy.　　他很快樂。(代名詞)
3. *That he is lazy* is a well-known fact.　　他懶惰是衆所週知的事實。(名詞子句：名詞相等語)
4. *Swimming* is his favorite sport.　　游泳是他所喜愛的運動。(動名詞：名詞相等語)
5. *To save money* is important.　　儲蓄是重要的事。(不定詞片語：名詞相等語)

(2)受詞

　　「**受詞**」是句子中動詞的「受事者」，也就是受到動詞所表示的動作所影響的人或事物。受詞由名詞、代名詞、或名詞相等語表示。

　　注意：如受詞爲代名詞時，要用受格形式。例如：

1. We saw *Larry*.　　我們看見 Larry。(名詞)
2. Tom bought two *books*.　　Tom 買了兩本書。(名詞)
3. I like *her*.　　我喜歡她。(代名詞)
4. I think (*that*) *she is happy*.　　我認爲她很快樂。(名詞子句：名詞相等語)
5. We like *jogging*.　　我們喜歡慢跑。(動名詞：名詞相等語)

6. Tom wanted *to leave.*　Tom 想離開。(不定詞: 名詞相等語)

注意: (a)介詞後面的名詞或代名詞叫做介詞的受詞。要用受格。例如:

7. He bought a ring for *her.*　他買了一只戒指給她。

　　(b)有些動詞如 give、buy 等可帶兩個受詞，其中直接受動作所
　　　影響的一個受詞叫做「直接受詞」，另一個則叫做「間接受詞」。
　　　例如:

8. She gave *me a book.*　她給我一本書。(book 為直接受詞, me
　為間接受詞)

(3)修飾語

「**修飾語**」泛指一切修飾另一語詞的單字、片語、或子句。包括最常用的
形容詞及副詞, 另外, 「**補語**」(complement)及「**同位語**」(appositive)也是
修飾語。以下例句中, 斜體部分是修飾語, 箭號所指為被修飾的語詞:

1. Jane has a *red* dress .　Jane 有一件紅洋裝。(形容詞)

2. The boy spoke *loudly.*　那個男孩大聲地說話。(副詞)

3. The man looked *angry.*　那個男人看起來很生氣。(主詞補語)

4. Peter is a *doctor.*　Peter 是醫生。(主詞補語)

5. We elected him *president.*　我們選他為總統。(受詞補語)

6. Jane, *my daughter*, is a nurse.　我的女兒 Jane 是護士。(同
　位語)

7. The book *on the desk* is mine.　桌子上的那本書是我的。(介
　詞片語: 作形容詞用)

8. He worked *for a long time.*　他做事做了很久。(介詞片語:

作副詞用)

9. I like the camera *that he bought yesterday.* 我喜歡他昨天買的那部照相機。(關係子句: 作形容詞用)

10. *When Peter is nervous,* he speaks very fast. Peter 緊張時, 說話說得很快。(副詞子句)

《習題 4》

(A)在下列各句中, 將主詞及受詞選出, 並分別註明。

　例: *John* saw *the boy.*
　　　主詞　　　受詞

1. Tom was lying on the floor.
2. My teacher bought a new book yesterday.
3. She bought a doll for her sister.
4. Morton gave her a present.
5. We can see a lot of trees in the park.
6. The telephone is a useful tool.
7. A man walked into Mr. Wang's office.
8. What did you see?
9. Please open the door.
10. Our teacher loves flowers.

(B)在下列各句中, 將修飾語選出, 並以箭號標示被修飾的語詞。

　例: This is a *good* book.
　　　They ran *fast.*

Tom went *upstairs in a hurry.*

1. Please stand here.

2. Tom is walking slowly.

3. We can speak simple English.

4. Tom seemed happy.

5. They are my good friends.

6. He was absent yesterday because he was ill.

7. The boy who is sitting next to Mary can run very fast.

8. Bob, my cousin, is a very tall boy.

第四章
句型略要

4.1. 句子的基本部分：主詞與述語　

　　英語的句子分爲「主詞」與「述語」兩大部分。主詞爲句子談論的主題，而述語則爲有關這主題的訊息。形式上，主詞爲名詞、代名詞或名詞相等語，述語則是主詞以外的部分。試看以下各句的分析：

主詞	述語
The sun	is shining.
John	hit Mary.
Mary	gave Tom a book.
The man	seemed happy.
We	kept our shoes dry.
The book on the desk	is mine.

4.2.　句子的核心

在構成句子的各種結構及語詞中，**動詞是最重要的字**，因爲動詞是述語的核心，也是**句子語意的要素**。一般說來，除感嘆句外，一個句子必須有一個完整的述語動詞。

因此，句型的分類，往往以動詞以及在述語中與動詞連用的其他語詞爲基準。在下面第 4.3.節列出英語的基本句型之前，我們要指出，**英語動詞分爲「及物動詞」**(transitive verb)**及「不及物動詞」**(intransitive verb)兩種。及物動詞後面要有受詞，不及物動詞後面則不帶受詞。

4.3.　基本句型

英語句型的基本形式並不多，用最概括的方式分類起來，有五種。有些文法書會依動詞的次分類把句型細分爲十至十幾種。但是，對中國學生而言，分類太多太細不易記憶及理解，學習效果反而不好。

在說明基本句型之前，爲方便起見，我們先介紹一些常用的文法術語的略寫：

　　　　Subj.＝Subject　　　主詞
　　　　Pred.＝Predicate　　　述語
　　　　NP＝Noun Phrase　　　名詞組(名詞片語)
　　　　VP＝Verb Phrase　　　動詞組(動詞片語)
　　　　Obj.＝Object　　受詞
　　　　Vt＝Transitive Verb　　　及物動詞

Vi＝Intransitive Verb　不及物動詞

V-ing＝Present Participle／Gerund（Verb in ing-form）
　　　ing 形式(現在分詞／動名詞)

V-ed＝Past form of Verb　動詞過去式

V-en＝Past Participle　過去分詞

Adj.＝Adjective／Adjectival　形容詞／形容詞結構

Adv.＝Adverb／Adverbial　副詞／副詞結構

Comp.＝Complement　補語

Obj. Comp.＝Object Complement　受詞補語

Subj. Comp.＝Subject Complement　主詞補語

D.O.＝Direct Object　直接受詞

I.O.＝Indirect Object　間接受詞

N＝Noun　名詞

V＝Verb　動詞

Prep.＝Preposition　介詞

Conj.＝Conjunction　連接詞

Art.＝Article　冠詞

Aux.＝Auxiliary　助動詞

Interj.＝Interjection　感嘆詞

Sing.＝Singular　單數

Pl.＝Plural　複數

Part.＝Particle　介副詞

(1)句型 1

Subj.＋Vi

Subj.主詞	Pred.述語
NP 名詞組	Vi 不及物動詞

注意: NP 指名詞、代名詞及名詞相等語，以下各句型中亦如此。
例如:

    1. It was raining.　當時正在下雨。

    2. They have left.　他們離開了。

    3. Birds fly.　鳥兒會飛。

不及物動詞後不能帶受詞，但可帶副詞或副詞結構。例如:

    4. It rained yesterday.　昨天下雨。

    5. They left in a hurry.　他們匆忙地離開了。

    6. She arrived on time.　她準時到達。

(2)句型 2

Subj.＋Vi＋Subj. Comp.

Subj.主詞	Pred.述語	
NP 名詞組	Vi 不及物動詞　Subj. Comp.主詞補語	

這句型中的 Vi 指「連繫動詞」(linking verb)。其中包括 be、appear、become、feel、grow、look、remain、seem、smell、sound、stay、taste 等。

這句型中的補語可以是 NP、Adj.、Adv.、或介詞片語。以下例句中，斜體部分爲主詞補語。

1. Tim is a *student.*　Tim 是學生。

2. Larry was *tired.*　Larry 很累。

3. The television is *on.*　電視開了。

4. We are *in love.*　我們戀愛了。

5. Our car is *in the garage.*　我們的車子在車庫裏。

6. Steve became *angry.*　Steve 生氣了。

7. They seemed *happy.*　他們似乎很快樂。

8. We all felt *sorry.*　我們都覺得很抱歉。

9. The milk tastes *sour.*　這牛奶嚐起來是酸的。

10. She feels *at home.*　她覺得很自在。

(3)句型 3

Subj.＋Vt＋Obj.

Subj.主詞	Pred.述語	
NP 名詞組	Vt 及物動詞	Obj. 受詞
		NP 名詞組

本句型中，動詞後面之 NP 稱爲受詞，是直接受動詞所影響的人或事、

物。如受詞爲代名詞，應用受格形式(如 me、him、them、her、us 等)。
❶例如：

    1. The boy kicked the ball.　那個男孩子踢了那個球。

    2. We all know him.　我們都認識他。

    3. She bought some apples.　她買了些蘋果。

   注意：本句型的動詞包括上面的單字動詞，以及片語動詞(phrasal
         verb)，亦即是**動詞＋介副詞**的詞組。

    4. She *turned on* the radio.　她打(扭)開收音機。

    5. I *took off* my shirt.　我脫下我的襯衫。

    6. They *are looking for* you.　他們正在找你。

---

❶有些動詞(如 have、cost、weigh、lack、fit、equal 等)後面接 NP，但這些 NP 的功
能介於受詞與副詞之間。這些動詞在字典中亦歸類爲「及物動詞」。然而, 這些動詞(有些
文法書稱之爲 Middle Verbs「中間動詞」)與眞正的及物動詞不同之處是, 眞正的及物
動詞可以有被動式, 但這些動詞則不可。例如: 我們可以說 John hit Tom. (John 打
了 Tom), 也可以說 Tom was hit by John.(Tom 被 John 打了)。但是, I have two
dollars.(我有兩塊錢), 却不可以說成*Two dollars are had by me. The book
costs thirty dollars.(這本書價值三十塊錢), 也不可以說成*Thirty dollars are cost
by the book.

　　含有這類動詞的句子在有些文法書中會認爲是另一種句型; 但本書不另外處理, 因爲
其結構基本上仍是 NP＋VP＋NP。然而, 我們必須記住, 這些中間動詞後面之 NP 與
一般受詞不同, 不可以有被動式。其他的例子如:

　　He ran a mile.　他跑了一英里。

　　Dan lacks confidence.　Dan 缺乏信心。

　　Two times two equals four.　二乘二等於四。

⑷句型 4

Subj.＋Vt＋I.O.＋D.O.

Subj.主詞	Pred.述語		
		I.O.間接受詞	D.O.直接受詞
NP 名詞組	Vt 及物動詞	NP 名詞組	NP 名詞組

　　英語中有些動詞如 ask、give、buy、send、show、build、choose、do、find、get、leave、order、prepare、save 等, 可以有兩個受詞, 一個稱爲直接受詞(通常爲事、物), 另一個稱爲間接受詞(通常爲人或動物)。當然, 這兩個受詞都是受格, 如爲代名詞, 則得用受格形式。例如:

　　1. I gave <u>*him*</u> <u>*a book.*</u>　我給他一本書。
　　　　　　I.O.　D.O.

　　2. He sent <u>*Mary*</u> <u>*some flowers.*</u>　他送一些花給 Mary。
　　　　　　　I.O.　　D.O.

　　3. They bought <u>*me*</u> <u>*a present.*</u>　他們給我買了一份禮物。
　　　　　　　　I.O.　D.O.

　　這句型可以變成 Subj.＋Vt＋D.O.＋Prep.＋I.O.(即主詞＋及物動詞＋直接受詞＋介詞＋間接受詞), 其語意不變。例如:

　　4. I gave a book to him.

　　5. He sent some flowers to Mary.

　　6. They bought a present for me.

這個相關的句型中的介詞大多數都用 to, 但動詞如爲 buy 或 make

時，介詞用 for；動詞爲 ask 時，介詞用 of。例如：

7. $\left\{\begin{array}{l}\text{Mother made a cake for me.} \\ \text{Mother made me a cake.}\end{array}\right.$

媽媽爲我做了一個蛋糕。

8. $\left\{\begin{array}{l}\text{He asked a favor of me.} \\ \text{He asked me a favor.}\end{array}\right.$

他請我幫忙。

(5)句型 5

Subj.＋Vt＋Obj.＋Obj. Comp.

Subj.主詞	Pred.述語		
NP 名詞組	Vt 及物動詞	Obj.受詞	Obj. Comp. 受詞補語
		NP 名詞組	$\left\{\begin{array}{l}\text{NP 名詞組} \\ \text{Adj.形容詞}\end{array}\right.$

本句型之受詞後面接一個修飾受詞的補語，稱爲「**受詞補語**」(object complement)。**如動詞爲 consider、think、find、make 等，受詞補語可以是 NP 或 Adj.；如動詞爲 appoint、call、elect、name、choose 等，受詞補語只能用 NP**。例如：(斜體部分爲受詞補語)

1. We consider him *a good friend.*　我們認爲他是個好朋友。

2. I thought her *clever.*　我覺得她聰明。

3. He thinks himself *a good student.*　他覺得自己是個好學生

4. We find him *a bore.*　我們發覺他是個無聊的人。

5. We find this book *very interesting.*　我們發現這本書很有趣。

6. Mr. Smith made Peter *his assistant.*　Smith 先生請 Peter 當他的助理。

7. You make me *sick.*　你令我覺得噁心。

8. We elected him *our president.*　我們選他為我們的總統。

9. They called me *a fool.*　他們稱我為傻瓜。

10. They named their baby *Paul.*　他們給他們的嬰兒取名為 Paul。

《習題 5》

(A)認識主詞與述語。在下面各句中，請在主詞與述語之間用一直線分開。注意：句子中的修飾語不影響被修飾之語詞的文法功能。

例：John ｜ is here.

　　John and Peter ｜ saw that boy.

　　The man wearing a red cap ｜ is my brother.

1. He is studying English.

2. They are soldiers.

3. We went swimming yesterday.

4. Alice bought me a new shirt.

5. The soup on the table smells good.

6. The man who is sitting over there is my uncle.

7. Tom said nothing for several minutes.

8. We played basketball yesterday.

9. He will look after you.

10. Tim can swim.

(B)將下列各句之主要部分分別以 Subj(主詞), Vi(不及物動詞), Vt(及物動詞), Obj(受詞), Subj. Comp.(主詞補語), Obj. Comp.(受詞補語), D.O.(直接受詞), I.O.(間接受詞)來標示。

    例： *John   is   here.*

        Subj. Vi Subj. Comp.

    John and Peter   saw   us.

        Subj.   Vt. Obj.

1. His father can swim.

2. You made me very happy.

3. Our teacher told us a story.

4. They elected (選) him monitor (班長) of the class.

5. Mother gave me two pieces of cake.

6. I wrote him a letter.

7. We will be late.

8. They enjoy jogging.

9. He is my brother.

10. I bought a present for him.

第五章
動詞的種類與形式

5.1. 動詞的種類(Verb Classes)

動詞可以分為「**普通動詞**」(ordinary verb)及「**助動詞**」(auxiliary verb)兩大類。普通動詞又可分為「及物動詞」(transitive verb)與「不及物動詞」(intransitive verb);而助動詞又可分為「主要助動詞」(primary auxiliaries)與「情態助動詞」(modal auxiliaries)兩種。我們可以用下頁的圖表示。

助動詞沒有詞形的變化,但普通動詞依照其過去式及過去分詞的詞形變化方式,再細分為「規則動詞」(regular verb)及「不規則動詞」(irregular verb)兩種。例如:

規則動詞	**不規則動詞**
ask (asked、asked)	hit (hit、hit)
stay (stayed、stayed)	send (sent、sent)
	swim (swam、swum)

(關於規則動詞及不規則動詞的詞形變化, 參看下面第 5.2. 之(3)節)。
普通動詞指一般的單字或片語動詞, 如 hit、swim、work、send、want、

look after(照顧)、turn off(關掉)、give up(放棄)等，其主要功能是表達「述語」的主要語意。例如：

　　1. He *came* here yesterday. 他昨天來這兒。

　　2. He *kicked* the ball. 他踢了那個球。

　　助動詞最主要的功能在「**幫助**」普通動詞構成一個完整的動詞組(verb phrase)，**以表示各種動詞結構形式**(如疑問式、否定式、被動式、進行式、完成式等)**以及「情態」**(如能力、可能性、義務、意願等)。

　　「幫助」普通動詞構成各種動詞結構形式的是「主要助動詞」Be、Have 及 Do。例如：

　　3. I *am* going to school now. 我現在正要上學去。(進行式)

　　4. I *have* finished doing my homework. 我已經做完功課。(完

成式)

　　5. These stories *are* called Aesop's Fables. 這些故事(被)稱爲
　　　伊索寓言。(被動式)

「幫助」普通動詞表達各種「情態」的是「**情態助動詞**」。另外, shall 與 will
也是構成將來式的助動詞。

　　6. He *can* help us. 他能幫助我們。(能力)

　　7. You *may* come in. 你可以進來。(允許)

　　8. It *may* rain this afternoon. 今天下午可能會下雨。(可能性)

　　9. We *should* get up early in the morning. 我們在早上應該一
　　　早起牀。(責任／義務)

　　10. I *must* see him now. 我必須現在見他。(需要)

　　另外, 在「問句」及「否定句」的形成過程中, 助動詞(包括主要助動詞及
情態助動詞)也扮演重要的功能。例如:

　　11. *Can* he come early? 他可以早到嗎?

　　12. *Do* you like this pen? 你喜歡這枝筆嗎?

　　13. I *don't* (= *do not*) want a book. 我不想要一本書。

　　14. He *cannot* swim. 他不會游泳。

5.2.　動詞的形式(Verb Forms)

　　英語的動詞除情態助動詞以外, 會因爲時式及主詞的人稱、數目等的不
同而有詞形的變化。

⑴主要助動詞 be、have、do

A. *Be*

	肯定式	否定式	否定略寫/讀式
原式	*be*		
-s(現在)形式	第一人稱 單數　　　　am, 'm	am not 'm not	*❶
	第三人稱 單數　　　　is, 's	is not 's not	isn't
	第二人稱單、 複數及第一、are, 're 三人稱複數	are not 're not	aren't
-ed(過去)形式	第一、三人稱 單數　　　　was	was not	wasn't
	第二人稱單、 複數及第一、were 三人稱複數	were not	weren't
-ing(現在分詞)形式	being		
-en(過去分詞)形式	been		

---

❶在一般用法中, am not 沒有略寫／讀式。但在英式英語裏, 否定疑問式 Am I
not?在口語中常用 Aren't I?來表示。在美式英語裏, ain't 可以表示 am not,
但 ain't 一般認為不是標準的用法。除此之外, ain't 還可以表示 isn't、aren't、
haven't、hasn't 之意。

B. *Have*

	肯定式	否定式	否定略寫/讀式
原式	*have*		
-s(現在)形式	第一、二人稱單、複數及第三人稱複數　have, 've	have not 've not	haven't
	第三人稱單數 has, 's	has not 's not	hasn't
-ed(過去)形式	had, 'd	had not 'd not	hadn't
-ing(現在分詞)形式	having		
-en(過去分詞)形式	had		

C. *Do*

	肯定式	否定式	否定略寫/讀式
原式	*do*		
-s(現在)形式	第一、二人稱單、複數及第三人稱複數　do	do not	don't
	第三人稱單數　does	does not	doesn't
-ed(過去)形式	did	did not	didn't
-ing(現在分詞)形式	doing		
-en(過去分詞)形式	done		

(2)情態助動詞

　　情態助動詞沒有詞形上的變化，第三人稱單數不加-s，也沒有現在或過去分詞的形式（例如沒有*cans 或*musting 的形式）。雖然在時式關聯並用時，would、could、should、might 可算是 will、can、shall、may 的過去形式；然而，除此以外，情態助動詞的確可以說是沒有字形上的變化。

(3)普通動詞

　　普通動詞如主詞是第三人稱單數，而時式是簡單現在式時，動詞要在原式後面加字尾-s；如時式為過去式時，詞形有規則與不規則之別，規則動詞在原式後面加字尾-ed，不規則動詞則有另外的字形變化形式；現在分詞則在原式後面加-ing；過去分詞也有規則與不規則之別，規則動詞的過去分詞和過去式一樣，在原式後面加-ed，不規則動詞則有另外的字形變化。

　　A.規則動詞(regular verbs)
　　規則動詞的過去式與過去分詞都是在原式後面加-ed 字尾而形成。第三人稱單數現在式在原式後面加-s 字尾；現在分詞則在原式後面加-ing。例如：

原式	-ed(過去)式	-en(過去分詞)式
work	worked	worked
want	wanted	wanted
等		

注意：(a)對普通動詞而言，無論是規則動詞或是不規則動詞，其第三人稱單數現在式與現在分詞，都是在原式後面分別加上-s 字尾及-ing 字尾而形成。因此一般文法書慣例都只列原式、-ed 形式、以及-en 形式。

(b)關於動詞加字尾時拼寫上應該注意事項, 參看第六章6.8.節。

B.不規則動詞

英語的不規則動詞只有三百個左右, 其中有些並不常用。因此, 雖然形式變化不規則, 但要把常用的熟記, 也不至於太難。我們常以其原式、-ed 形式及-en 形式之間之異同來分類(如 A─A─A 型, 即三式同式者), 以便記憶。以下我們列舉初學階段比較常用的不規則動詞。(關於所有不規則動詞的細節, 可參看編寫完善的字典所附的不規則動詞表)

(a)　第一型: A─A─A 型(原式, -ed 式及-en 式都相同)

原式	過去式(-ed)	過去分詞(-en)
bet　打賭	bet	bet
bid　出價	bid	bid
cost　值, 費	cost	cost
cut　切, 割	cut	cut
hit　打	hit	hit
hurt　傷害	hurt	hurt
let　讓	let	let
put　放	put	put
read [rid] 讀	read [rɛd]	read [rɛd]
set　安置	set	set
shut　關	shut	shut

(b)　第二型: A─B─A 型(原式與-en 式相同)

become　變成	became	become
come　來	came	come

原式	過去式(-ed)	過去分詞(-en)
run　跑	ran	run

(c)　第三型：A—B—B 型(-ed 式與-en 式相同)

bend　彎, 屈	bent／bended	bent／bended
bleed　流血	bled	bled
bring　帶來	brought	brought
build　建造	built	built
burn　燒	burnt／burned	burnt／burned
buy　買	bought	bought
catch　捕捉	caught	caught
creep　爬	crept	crept
dig　掘	dug	dug
dream　做夢	dreamed／dreamt	dreamed／dreamt
feed　餵, 養	fed	fed
feel　感覺	felt	felt
fight　打, 打仗	fought	fought
find　發現, 找	found	found
get　得	got	got (gotten)
hang　掛, 吊	hung	hung
have (has)　有	had	had
hear　聽	heard	heard
hold　拿, 握住	held	held
keep　保持	kept	kept
lay　放置, 產(卵)	laid	laid
lead　領導	led	led

原式	過去式(-ed)	過去分詞(-en)
learn　學習	learnt／learned	learnt／learned
leave　離開	left	left
lend　借	lent	lent
lose　遺失	lost	lost
make　做, 使	made	made
mean　意謂	meant	meant
meet　遇見	met	met
pay　付款	paid	paid
say　說	said	said
sell　賣	sold	sold
send　送, 寄	sent	sent
shoot　射擊	shot	shot
sit　坐	sat	sat
sleep　睡	slept	slept
smell　聞起來	smelt／smelled	smelt／smelled
spell　拼寫, 拼字	spelt／spelled	spelt／spelled
spend　花費, 耗費	spent	spent
stand　站	stood	stood
strike　打, 擊	struck	struck
sweep　掃	swept	swept
teach　教	taught	taught
tell　告訴	told	told
think　想	thought	thought
understand　明白	understood	understood
win　獲勝	won	won

原式	過去式(-ed)	過去分詞(-en)
wrap　包	wrapped／wrapt	wrapped／wrapt

(d)　第四型：A－B－C 型(原式，-ed 及-en 式都不同)

arise　起來	arose	arisen
begin　開始	began	begun
bite　咬	bit	bitten／bit
blow　吹	blew	blown
break　打破	broke	broken
choose　選擇	chose	chosen
do　做	did	done
draw　拉, 畫	drew	drawn
drive　駕駛	drove	driven
eat　吃	ate	eaten
fall　落下	fell	fallen
fly　飛	flew	flown
forget　忘記	forgot	forgotten／forgot
give　給	gave	given
go　去	went	gone
grow　生長	grew	grown
hide　躲, 藏	hid	hidden／hid
know　知道	knew	known
lie　躺	lay	lain
ride　騎	rode	ridden
ring　響, 鳴	rang	rung
see　看見	saw	seen

原式	過去式(-ed)	過去分詞(-en)
shake　搖動	shook	shaken
show　展示	showed	shown／showed
sing　唱	sang	sung
speak　說	spoke	spoken
steal　偷	stole	stolen
swim　游泳	swam	swum
take　拿	took	taken
throw　投, 擲	threw	thrown
wear　穿	wore	worn
write　寫	wrote	written

(e)　第五型: A—A—B 型(原式與-ed 式相同, 但-en 式不同)

beat　打	beat	beaten

5.3.　動詞組的結構(Structure of the Verb Phrase)

　　我們知道每一句子都必須有動詞。但是動詞可能是一個普通動詞, 也可能是包含助動詞及普通動詞的組合。因此, 對句子中的動詞我們都稱為句子的「**動詞組**」(verb phrase)。如動詞組只有一個普通動詞, 我們稱之為「**簡單動詞組**」(simple verb phrase), 如動詞組含有助動詞加普通動詞, 我們稱之為「**複合動詞組**」(complex verb phrase)。例如:

　　1. He *worked* hard.　他努力地工作。(簡單動詞組)

　　2. I *saw* him.　我看見他。(簡單動詞組)

　　3. John *has gone* home.　　John 已經回家去了。(複合動詞組)

4. They **should be working** hard.　他們應該努力地工作。(複
合動詞組)

複合動詞有四種基本形式:

A. 情態助動詞式: **情態助動詞＋動詞原式**

I **must go** now. 我現在必須走。

He **will come** later. 他過一會兒會來。

B. 完成式: Have＋**過去分詞**

She **has said** nothing. 她什麼都沒說。

I **have done** my homework. 我已經做完功課了。

C. 進行式: Be＋**現在分詞**

He **is eating** his breakfast. 他正在吃早餐。

Mary **is writing** a letter to her mother.　Mary 正在寫信給
她媽媽。

D. 被動式: Be＋**過去分詞**

The child **was beaten.** 這個小孩子被打了。

The thief **was caught**. 這小偷被捉了。

《習題 6》

(A)將下列句子中的動詞組找出來。

例: We <u>won</u> the game.

He <u>will come</u> tomorrow.

1. She opened the door.

2. No one is here.

3. It seldom rains here in October.

4. The letter was mailed yesterday.

5. Debby can sing very well.

6. George has done his homework.

7. We were late for the party last night.

8. Birds can fly.

9. They hope to visit Taiwan next month.

10. I was told about the good news this morning.

(B)將下列各句之動詞改爲過去式。

例: We _are_ happy.

　　We _were_ happy.

　　He _comes_ home.

　　He _came_ home.

1. Judy opens the door.

2. John prefers tea to coffee.

3. I make a cake for him.

4. They are tired.

5. Bill gets up early.

6. Tom does a good job.

7. He wants to buy that new book.

8. She leaves the house at 8:30.

9. It begins to rain.

10. We dig a hole in our garden.

11. I give him ten dollars.

12. She feels nervous.

(C)填入適當的動詞形式。

	原式	過去式	過去分詞
1.	come	came	come
2.	go	——	——
3.	——	ran	——
4.	hit	——	——
5.	——	——	bought
6.	bring	——	——
7.	dig	——	——
8.	get	——	——
9.	——	heard	——
10.	say	——	——
11.	——	sold	——
12.	——	——	stood
13.	——	——	begun
14.	forget	——	——
15.	write	——	——
16.	——	swam	——
17.	think	——	——

第六章
動詞的時式

6.1. 時間、時式、情狀(Time, Tense and Aspect)

「**時間**」(time)是一般的觀念，如過去、現在、將來。

「**時式**」(tense，有些文法書也稱之為「時態」)是英語動詞在文法上的一種形式，通常(但並不一定)表示動作所發生的時間。

「**情狀**」(aspect)是英語動詞所表達的動作的情形與狀態(例如：動作是否在進行中、或是已經完成了等等)。

英語的時式有三種：「現在式」(present)、「過去式」(past)、「將來式」(future)。

英語的情狀有三種：「進行狀」(progressive)、「完成狀」(perfect)、「完成進行狀」(perfect progressive)。

英語的時式與情狀可以互相配合，用來描述動詞動作在時間上以及情狀上的種種可能。在英語中，不與情狀組合的時式叫「簡單式」(simple tense)，分現在、過去、將來三種，其餘三種情狀與三種時式組合，可產生九種時式。因此，英語一共有十二種可能的時式，其名稱及形式分別列舉於下面6.2.節。

6.2. 時式的形式(Forms of Tenses)

　　我們以動詞 work '工作'(規則動詞)與 do '做'(不規則動詞)為例, 把英語的十二種時式的形式例舉如下:

現在式

簡單現在式　　　　　work／do
(Simple present)　 works／does(主詞為第三人稱單數時)

現在進行式　　　　　am
(Present progressive)　are　} working／doing
　　　　　　　　　　　is

現在完成式　　　　has
(Present perfect)　have } worked／done

現在完成進行式　　　　　　has
(Present perfect progressive)　have } been working／doing

過去式

簡單過去式
(Simple past)　　worked／did

過去進行式　　　was
(Past progressive)　were } working／doing

過去完成式
(Past perfect)　had worked／done

過去完成進行式
(Past perfect progressive)　had been working／doing

簡單將來式 will
(Simple future) shall } work／do

將來進行式 will
(Future progressive) shall } be working／doing

將來式

將來完成式 will
(Future perfect) shall } have worked／done

將來完成進行式 will
(Future perfect progressive) shall } have been working／doing

6.3. 簡單時式的用法(Uses of the Simple Tenses)

6.3.1. 簡單現在式(Simple Present Tense)

形式: 簡單現在式的主詞如果是第三人稱單數時(如 he、 she、 it、 John、Mary、the boy 等), 在動詞原式後面加字尾-s; 主詞為其他人稱或複數時, 則使用動詞原式表示。

用法:

⑴簡單現在式可表示現在的情形或狀況。這種用法多用於「非動作動詞」(如 be、seem 等), 常用的例子如:

A. 連繫動詞(linking verbs) be、seem、look 等

　　1. He *is* my teacher. 他是我的老師。

2. This lesson **seems** very easy.　這一課似乎很容易。

3. They **looked** happy.　他們看起來很快樂。

B. 感官動詞(verbs of perception) feel、taste、see、smell、hear 等

1. This soup **tastes** good.　這湯嚐起來味道很好。

2. The baby's **skin** feels smooth.　這嬰兒的皮膚摸起來很柔滑。

3. I **hear** him talking loudly.　我聽到他高聲說話。

4. I **see** two students sitting there.　我看見兩個學生坐在那兒。

注意：(a)如表示現在特意去看或聽某人或某事物時，我們用 listen to 及 look at(或 watch)，而時式則用現在進行式。例如：

He **is listening to** the radio.　他正在聽收音機。

I **am looking at** Mr. Wang.　我正在看著王先生。

(b)如 feel、taste、smell 當及物動詞使用時，要用現在進行式來表示現在的動作。例如：

My mother **is tasting** the soup.　母親正在嚐嚐湯的味道。

C. 表示精神狀態或情況的動詞(如 agree '同意'、believe '相信'、know '知道'、 prefer '偏愛'、 remember '記得'、 think '認為'、 want '想要'等)

1. I **know** (that) he is happy.　我知道他快樂。

2. She **prefers** to stay at home.　她比較喜歡待在家裏。

3. He **wants** an apple.　他想要一個蘋果。

D. 表示情緒狀況的動詞(如 care '關心'、hate '恨'、like '喜歡'、love '愛'等)

We all **like** Mr. Li.　我們都喜歡李先生。

E. 其他的非動作動詞(如 belong '屬於'、have '有'、mean '意謂'、 need '需要'等)

1. I *need* your help.　我需要你的幫忙。

2. She *has* two brothers.　她有兩個弟弟。

(2)簡單現在式表示一般(不變)的眞理。這些眞理過去是眞，現在及將來也是眞。

1. The sun *rises* in the east and *sets* in the west.　太陽從東邊升起，從西邊降下。

2. The earth *revolves* around the sun.　地球繞太陽而運行。

(3)簡單現在式表示習慣性的動作。句中因此常有頻率副詞修飾動詞。

1. He *goes* to school *every day*.　他每天都上學。

2. She *never goes* to the movies alone.　她從來都不獨自去看電影。

3. He *goes* to Hong Kong *every year*.　他每年都去香港。

4. Mary *usually has* breakfast at seven o'clock in the morning.　Mary 通常在早上七點鐘吃早餐。

(4)簡單現在式可以表示將來的動作或行動。這些句子中常連有表示將來的語詞。

1. The ship *leaves for* New York tomorrow.　船明天開赴紐約。

2. The race *takes place* next Sunday.　比賽下星期天舉行。

在時間或條件子句中，簡單現在式也可以表示將來的動作。例如：

3. I will call you when he *arrives*.　他到達時我就會通知你。

4. We will do it if you *pay* us.　你付錢的話，我們就會做這事。

(5)簡單現在式可用來報導歷史事實，或敍述故事。例如：

The king **comes** out of the palace, **addresses** the people, and **asks** them to stand behind him.　國王走出皇宮，對群衆講話，並且要求他們支持他。

6.3.2.　簡單過去式(Simple Past Tense)

形式：簡單過去式以動詞的過去式構成。
用法：

(1)簡單過去式表示在過去某一時間發生的動作或情況。通常會與明確的時間語詞一起使用。

　1. She **saw** me yesterday.　她昨天看見我。

　2. He **left** two hours ago.　他兩個鐘頭前走了。

注意：有時候，句子中雖然沒有提到過去的時間，但動作很清楚地是在過去某一時間發生，我們也用簡單過去式(問句也是如此)。

　3. Tom **was** late.　Tom(當時)遲到了。

　4. When **did** he **leave**?　他什麼時候離開的?

　5. I **bought** this bicycle in Taipei.　我在臺北買了這輛腳踏車。

(2)簡單過去式表示在過去某一段時間的動作或行爲。

　1. She **lived** in Tainan for twenty years and then she **decided** to move to Taipei.　她在臺南住了二十年然後決定搬到臺北。

　2. He **studied** at Harvard University from 1976 to 1980. 他在1976 至 1980 年間在哈佛大學唸書。

⑶簡單過去式可表示過去的習慣或重覆發生的動作。句子中因此常有頻率副詞修飾動詞。

1. When I was a child, I *went* swimming *every Sunday*.
   我小時候每個星期天都去游泳。

2. It *rained* quite *frequently* in December last year.　去年十二月裏經常下雨。

過去習慣或重覆發生的動作也可以用 used to＋V 來表示。

3. When she was young, she *used to go* swimming *every Sunday*.　她小時候每星期天都去游泳。

⑷簡單過去式可用於表示假設的 if 子句，以及在 wish 後面的 that 子句中。但這種用法中的過去動詞並不是眞的過去動作。

1. If I *studied* hard now, I would pass the exam.　如果我現在用功唸書，我考試就會及格。

2. He wishes that he *were* rich.　他希望他有錢。(事實上他並不富有)

6.3.3.　簡單將來式(Simple Future Tense)

形式：**will／shall＋動詞原形**

(注意：傳統文法認爲第一人稱用 shall，第二、三人稱用 will。但在現代英語[特別是美式英語]中，並不很正確。在美式英語裏，無論甚麼人稱都可用 will。)

用法：

⑴簡單將來式表示將來的動作、行爲或情況。

　1. He *will be* seventeen next month.　下個月他就十七歲了。

　2. They *will come* here tomorrow.　他們明天會到這兒來。

　3. Don't worry, I *will help* her.　別擔心，我會幫助她的。

　4. We *won't go* to New York next week.　我們下週不會去紐
　　約。

⑵簡單將來式可表示動詞的意向。

　1. I *will see* you tomorrow.　我打算明天見你。

　2. Mary *will do* the work herself.　Mary 打算親自做這工作。

⑶簡單將來式可表示將來的習慣動作或經常會發生的行動。

　1. Summer *will come* again.　夏天會再來。

　2. She *will visit* us every year.　她每年都會來探望我。

⑷ be going to＋動詞也常用來表示簡單將來式。

　1. I *am going to see* you tomorrow.

　　（＝I will see you tomorrow.）

　2. They *are going to come* here tomorrow.

　　（＝They will come here tomorrow.）

⑸ shall 在現代英語中，常用於以下情形：

　1.提建議：*Shall* we *take* a taxi? 我們坐計程車好嗎?

　2.用於 let's 後面的附加短問句：Let's go, *shall* we? 我們走吧，
　　好嗎?

《習題7》

(A)將下列各句中的動詞以簡單現在式寫出。注意主詞的單複數。

1. He often _____ (go) to school by bus.

2. They usually _____ (stay) at school after classes.

3. I usually _____ (get) up early.

4. Larry _____ (dream) every night.

5. She always _____ (wear) a blue skirt.

6. Mary _____ (be) never late.

7. Noel _____ (speak) English very well.

8. He _____ (know) Robert very well.

9. Birds _____ (fly).

10. The cake _____ (smell) good.

11. Hens _____ (lay) eggs.

12. She _____ (think) we _____ (be) happy.

(B)將下列各句之動詞以簡單過去式寫出。

1. We _____ (have) a good time at the party last night.

2. Candy _____ (drive) too fast this afternoon.

3. The telephone _____ (ring) a few minutes ago.

4. We _____ (take) the wrong bus.

5. They _____ (pay) me two dollars.

6. We _____ (win) the game yesterday.

7. She _____ (tell) me an interesting story.

8. Edward _____ (fall) off the horse yesterday and _____ (break) his left leg.

(C)將下列各句之動詞以簡單將來式寫出。

1. Tom _____ (arrive) at eight o'clock.

2. I _____ (send) you a postcard when I arrive in New York.

3. Do you think he _____ (get) the job?

4. They _____ (visit) Taiwan next month.

5. Don't worry. He _____ (be) on time.

6. If I go shopping, I _____ (buy) some bananas for you.

7. I _____ (talk) to Mr. Wang about our plan tomorrow.

(D)填入簡單現在式或簡單過去式。

1. The airplane _____ (fly) over our school yesterday.

2. How often _____ you _____ (go) to the supermarket?

3. Usually, I _____ (not, like) lazy students.

4. A jumble jetliner(巨無霸噴射客機)_____ (carry) a lot of passengers.

5. We _____ (win) the game last Tuesday.

6.4.　進行時式的用法(Uses of the Progressive Tenses)

6.4.1.　現在進行式(Present Progressive Tense)

形式: am／are／is＋V-ing

用法:

⑴表示現在正在做(進行中)的動作。

　　1. What *are* you *doing* here?　你在這兒幹什麼?

　　2. I *am writing* a letter to my father.　我正在寫信給父親。

⑵現在進行式可表示預先安排好而很快就要進行的事或行動,這種用法常與表示將來時間的副詞連用。

　　1. He *is giving* a lecture next Tuesday.　下星期二他要演講。

　　2. I *am meeting* Mr. Smith tomorrow.　我明天會見 Smith 先生。

6.4.2.　通常不用於進行時式的動詞(Verbs Not Normally Used in the Progressive Tenses)

進行時式主要用於動作動詞, 非動作動詞通常不用於進行時式。非動作動詞如要表示現在時, 用簡單現在式。這些不用於進行時式的動詞有以下幾種:

⑴連繫動詞: be '是'、seem '似乎'、appear '似乎、看來'、look '看來'等。(例句參看6.3.1.⑴A.)

⑵感官動詞: feel '感覺起來'、taste '嚐起來'、smell '聞起來'、see '看見'、hear '聽見'等。(例句參看6.3.1.⑴B.)

⑶表示精神情況的動詞: agree '同意'、believe '相信'、know '知道'、prefer '偏愛'、remember '記得'、think '認爲'、want '想要'等。(例句參看6.3.1.⑴C.)

⑷表示情緒狀況的動詞: care '關心'、hate '恨'、like '喜歡'、love '愛'等。(例句參看6.3.1.⑴D.)

(5)其他非動作動詞: have '有'、belong '屬於'、mean '意謂'、need '需要'等。(例句參看6.3.1.(1)E.)

以上五類動詞通常不用於進行式。但表示特意的動作時,則可用進行式。例如:

(1) see 表示「看見」(感官功能)時不能用進行式, 但表示「接見」、「面談」時則可:

The manager *is seeing* the applicants tomorrow.　經理明天要與申請人面談。

(2) hear 表示「聽見」(感官功能)時不能用進行式, 但表示「聽證」或「收到信息」時則可:

The court *is hearing* evidence next Monday.　法庭下週一聽取證詞。

I hope I *will be hearing* from you soon.　我希望很快會收到你的來信。

(3) feel 表示「感覺起來」(感官動詞)時不能用進行式, 但表示「觸摸」時則可:

He *is feeling* the surface of the desk.　他正在用手去觸摸桌子的表面。

(4) taste 表示東西的味道「嚐起來」如何(感官功能)時, 不能用進行式, 但表示某人特意去「嚐試味道」時則可:

Mother *is tasting* the soup.　媽媽正在嚐嚐湯的味道。

(5) smell 表示東西的氣味「聞起來」如何(感官動詞)時, 不能用進行式, 但表示某人特意去「聞」某些東西的味道時則可:

Why *are* you *smelling* the soup? Does it *smell* good?　你為什麼要聞一聞這湯呢? 聞起來還好吧?

(6) look 表示事物或情況「看起來」如何(連繫動詞)時, 不能用進行式,

但與介(副)詞連用表示特意的動作時(如 look at '看'、look for '找尋'等)則可用進行式：

I am **looking at** her. 我正在看著她。

He **is looking for** a new job. 他正在找一份新的工作。

(7) think 表示「認爲」(精神狀態, 說話者的意見)時, 不能用進行式, 但表示「想」時則可。試比較：

I **think** you are right. 我認爲你是對的。(不能說*I am thinking you are right.)

但 What **are** you **thinking** about? 你正在想些什麼？

6.4.3. 過去進行式(Past Progressive Tense)

形式：was／were＋V-ing

用法：

⑴過去進行式表示在過去某時間正在進行的動作。通常含有表示過去時間的副詞。

1. She **was writing** a letter at noon. 中午的時候她正在寫信。

2. She **was doing** her homework all morning last Sunday. 她上星期天整個上午都在做功課。

⑵過去進行式表示在過去某一個動作發生時(用簡單過去表示), 另一動作(用過去進行式表示)正在進行之中。用簡單式動詞表示的動作通常比較短暫。

1. When I **arrived**, they **were having** lunch. 我到達時他們正在吃午飯。

2. She *was taking* a bath when the phone rang.　電話鈴響時她正在洗澡。

3. While I *was writing* a letter, I heard the phone ring.　當我在寫信時, 我聽到電話鈴響。

6.4.4.　將來進行式 (Future Progressive Tense)

形式: will／shall＋be＋V-ing

用法:

(1)將來進行式表示在將來某一段或某一點時間將要進行的動作。

1. He *will be helping* us tomorrow.　他明天將會幫我們。

2. A: What *will* you *be doing* at six tomorrow morning?　明天早上六點你將會在做什麼?

　B: I *'ll be having* my breakfast.　我將會正在吃早餐。

(2)將來進行式常與類似 soon 的時間副詞連用, 表示很快就要進行的動作。

1. I *will be working* for Mr. Wang soon.　我很快就會替王先生做事了。

2. Very soon we *will be writing* to you.　我們很快就會寫信給你。

《習題 8》

(A)用現在、過去、及將來三種進行時式來重寫下列句子。

　例：I work hard.

　　　I am working hard.

　　　I was working hard.

　　　I will／shall be working hard.

1. She plans to buy a house.

2. Bob stays at a hotel.

3. I try to study hard.

4. Some friends help me.

5. The bells of the church ring.

6. He throws a stone at the dog.

7. We go to the movies.

(B)下列各句中，選用簡單現在式或現在進行式。

1. The sun _____ (rise) in the east.

2. Right now I _____ (study) English grammar.

3. Listen! The bells of the church _____ (ring).

4. We _____ (celebrate 慶祝) the Dragon Boat Festival (端午節) once a year.

5. He _____ (play) tennis now.

6. It _____ (get) warmer and warmer.

7. She _____ (play) tennis better than you.

8. He usually _____ (get) up at 6:30 in the morning.

9. _____ you _____ (belong) to this club (俱樂部)?

10. Why _____ you _____ (look) at me like that? Do I look funny?

(C)下列各句中，選用簡單過去式或過去進行式。

1. Our project (計劃)＿＿＿＿ (begin) in 1987.

2. He ＿＿＿＿ (go) there on time, didn't he?

3. We ＿＿＿＿ (wash) the dishes when you ＿＿＿＿ (come) to see us.

4. Tom ＿＿＿＿ (see) me twice last week.

5. I ＿＿＿＿ (wash) my clothes when I saw Mr. Johnson.

6. The tourist (觀光客)＿＿＿＿ (lose) his way while he ＿＿＿＿ (walk) around the downtown area (城中鬧區).

7. At 7:30 last night I ＿＿＿＿ (watch) TV.

8. Peter ＿＿＿＿ (take) a photo of me while I was not looking at the camera (照相機).

9. I ＿＿＿＿ (have) no idea of what he ＿＿＿＿ (do) at that time.

10. I ＿＿＿＿ (see) John there this morning.

6.5. 完成時式的用法 (Uses of the Perfect Tenses)

6.5.1. 現在完成時式 (Present Perfect Tense)

形式: have／has＋V-en (過去分詞)

用法:

⑴現在完成式表示剛完成的動作，常與 just 連用。

  1. She *has* just *left*. 她剛離開。

  2. We *have* just *finished* writing our report. 我們剛寫好我

們的報告。

注意：just now 的意思是「不久以前」，只能用於簡單過去式，不能與現在完成式連用。

(2)現在完成式表示最近才完成但現在仍然有效果的動作。

1. I *have read* this book.　我已經讀完這本書了。

2. He *has washed* his car and it looks very nice.　他已經洗過他的車子，車子現在看起來很不錯了。

3. It *has been* very hot lately.　最近天氣一直都很熱。

4. He *has lived* in Taipei for three years.　他在臺北已經住了三年。

5. I *have smoked* since 1980.　自從 1980 年以來我就抽菸了。

6. She *has not felt* well since she had a cold last week.　自從上星期感冒以來，她就一直不舒服。

7. I *have been* very busy lately.　我最近一直都很忙。

注意：因爲現在完成式所表示的動作的時間並不確定,因此表示明確的過去某一個時間的副詞如 yesterday, two minutes ago, at five o'clock 等等不可以與現在完成式連用。但表示不明確時間的副詞如 lately'最近', before '從前'、always '一向'等，以及表示一段時間的副詞如 for three years '三年'、up to now '到目前爲止'、since 1970 '從 1970 年以來' 等等, 則可與現在完成式連用。(參看以上例句 3 至 7)

(3)現在完成式表示說話者的經驗。類似 ever '從來'、never '從未、不'、often '常常'等頻率副詞常用來修飾動詞。

1. *Have* you ever *seen* a ghost?　你見過鬼嗎？

2. I *have* never *seen* a kangaroo.　我從來沒有看過袋鼠。

3. She *has been* to New York several times.　她到過紐約好幾次了。

(4)現在完成式與簡單現在式應注意的事項。

A.句子中有明確表示過去某個時間的詞語時，不能用現在完成式，只能用簡單過去式，因爲現在完成式動作起始時間並不清楚。因此，我們不可以說*I have seen him yesterday.，我們只能說 I saw him yesterday.

B. for 與 since：「since＋某個時間」只與現在完成式連用。一般說來「for＋一段時間」通常也是與現在完成式連用。

1. I *have studied* English since I was ten.　我從十歲開始就學英文了。

2. She *has lived* here for ten years.　她在這兒住了十年了。(現在仍住在此)

但是，如果確知動作已經沒有現在效果時，「for＋一段時間」也可以與簡單過去式連用。

3. He *was* in the army for 3 years.　他在部隊裏待過三年。(現在已經退伍了)

6.5.2.　過去完成式(Past Perfect Tense)

形式: had＋V-en(**過去分詞**)
用法:

過去完成式表示一個發生於過去某一時間(以時間副詞表示)或過去某一動作(以簡單過去式動詞表示)之前的動作。因此，過去完成式最常見的用

法是與簡單過去式配合使用，以簡單過去式表示過去某個時間的動作，而過去完成式則表示比這過去動作發生得更早的動作。

1. She *told* me that Tom *had bought* a new house.　她告訴我 Tom 已經買了一幢新房子。(「買」[had bought] 的動作先於「告訴」[told] 的動作)

2. He *said* that he *had left* his key at home.　他說他把鑰匙留在家裏。(「had left」在先，「said」在後)

3. We *had* already *eaten* our dinner when she *arrived*.　當她到達時我們早已吃過晚飯了。(「had eaten」在先，「arrived」在後)

6.5.3.　將來完成式(Future Perfect Tense)

形式：will／shall＋have＋V-en(**過去分詞**)
用法：

將來完成式主要表示一個在將來某一時間之前將會發生的動作。

1. By the end of next month he *will have lived* here for two years.　到了下月底他將會在這兒住滿兩年了。

2. Before the vacation is over, we *will have spent* all our money.　在假期結束以前我們將會把所有的錢都花光了。

6.6. 完成進行時式的用法（Uses of the Perfect Progressive Tenses）

6.6.1. 現在完成進行式（Present Perfect Progressive Tense）

形式: have／has＋been＋V-ing

用法:

現在完成進行式主要用來表示一直繼續到現在的動作。基本上現在完成進行式與現在完成式很相似，只是現在完成進行式強調動作之持續不斷。

1. He **has been watching** TV since six o'clock.　從六點開始他就一直看電視。

2. He **has been working** here for five years.　他在此地一直工作了五年。

6.6.2. 過去完成進行式（Past Perfect Progressive Tense）

形式: had＋been＋V-ing

用法:

過去完成進行式與過去完成式很相似,但比較強調動作的持續不斷的性質。

1. He **had been working** on his own farm for five years before he came to work for us.　在他來爲我們做事以前，他

一直在他自己的農場上工作了五年。

2. The doctor told him to take a few days off because he **had been working** too hard.　因為他一直工作得太辛勞了，醫生吩咐他休假幾天。

6.6.3.　將來完成進行式(Future Perfect Progressive Tense)

形式：will／shall＋have＋been＋V-ing

用法：

將來完成進行式用法與將來完成式相似，但強調動作的持續不斷的性質。

1. By the end of this semester he **will have been teaching** English for thirty years.　到本學期結束的時候，他將會一直不斷地教了三十年的英文了。

2. By eight o'clock this evening he **will have been watching** TV for ten hours.　到今天晚上八點，他將會一直不斷地看了十個鐘頭的電視了。

《習題 9》

(A)表示將來時間有以下幾種方式。

例：a　簡單將來式／將來進行式

b　簡單現在式

c　現在進行式

　　d　be going to＋V

將下列各句盡量以不同的表示將來時間的時式寫出。

例：(a) We will go to Taipei tomorrow.

　　　　We will be going to Taipei tomorrow.

　　　　We go to Taipei tomorrow.

　　　　We are going to Taipei tomorrow.

　　　　We are going to go to Taipei tomorrow.

　　(b) He will visit us.

　　　　He will be visiting us.

　　　　He is going to visit us.

1. I will see you later.

2. They will send me a letter.

3. He will come to my office tomorrow.

4. I will be here on Sunday morning.

5. She will make a cake for us.

(B)在下列各句中, 選用現在完成式或簡單過去式。

1. I _____ (stay) at the hotel since I got here.

2. The president _____ (die) a few months ago.

3. I _____ (see) him before. He looks quite familiar to me.

4. He _____ (work) for my uncle last summer.

5. I _____ (already, pay) the bill for you.

6. Thirty years ago, more people _____ (live) on farms.

7. I _____ (pay) my rent (房租) last Monday.

(C)在下列各句中, 選用簡單過去式或過去完成式。

1. When they _____ (finish) doing their homework, they left the house.

2. After Tom _____ (eat) his breakfast, he felt much better.

3. He thanked me because I _____ (help) him.

4. The woman who _____ (promise) to come did not show up(出現).

5. I _____ (know) that he had left the house.

6. By the time they got to the station, the train _____ (leave).

7. Terry said that his mother _____ (give) him a million dollars.

8. He _____ (be) happy because we had just told him the good news.

(D)在下列各句中，選用現在進行式、過去進行式、或將來進行式。

1. Mary _____ (read) a book now.

2. I _____ (work) for Mr. Long next month.

3. I _____ (eat) dinner when I heard Mr. Pike coming in.

4. Look!　John _____ (come) toward us.

5. I cannot come tomorrow because I _____ (study) English.

6. My mother _____ (make) a cake right now.

(E)在下列各句中，選用現在完成式、過去完成式、或將來完成式。

1. I _____ (be) to Japan many times before.

2. She _____ (never, see) a panda (貓熊).

3. I wasn't hungry because I _____ (just, eat) breakfast.

4. This is the best novel (小說) I _____ (ever, read).

5. I _____ (finish) writing this book by December next year.

6. The house was very quiet because everyone _____ (go) to bed.

7. Our teacher _____ (teach) English for twenty years by the end of this semester (學期).

(F)在下列各句中，使用適當的時式。

1. Cats _____ (like) fish.

2. He _____ (look) at the watch now.

3. The teacher _____ (tell) us a story yesterday.

4. The new stamps _____ (be) available next week.

5. The wind usually _____ (blow) from the north in winter.

6. By this time next week they _____ (receive) our letter.

7. I _____ (not, like) going to the movies very much.

8. The policeman _____ (walk) along the street when he saw the accident.

9. I _____ (already, sign) the paper (文件) when the lawyer arrived.

10. I _____ (receive) only one letter from him since he went away.

11. He _____ (wait) for Mr. Kaplan since two o'clock in the afternoon.

12. You _____ (get) there in time if you start running now.

6.7. 動詞變化拼寫應注意事項（Some Rules for the Spelling of Verbs）

　　動詞加-ing 或-ed 字尾時，在拼寫上有些應注意的事項。以下把重要的規則列舉出來，通常同一規則往往同時適用於加-ed 及加-ing 的形式：

(1)大部分動詞加-ed 及加-ing 時不需要作拼寫上的變化。

原式	過去式	過去分詞	現在分詞
act	acted	acted	acting
ask	asked	asked	asking

borrow	borrowed	borrowed	borrowing
cook	cooked	cooked	cooking
wash	washed	washed	washing

(2)動詞字尾為**字母** e，則過去式及過去分詞只加 d；而 e 如果不發音，現在分詞在加-ing 前要把 e 刪除。

like	liked	liked	liking
love	loved	loved	loving
(come	came	come	coming)

但注意：(a)如字尾為 ee 或 ye，現在分詞只加-ing，不把 e 刪去。

| agree | agreed | agreed | agreeing |
| (see | saw | seen | seeing) |

　　　(b)如字尾為 ie，現在分詞則將 ie 改為 y，再加-ing。

die	died	died	dying
lie	lied	lied	lying
tie	tied	tied	tying

(3)字尾為「**子音＋y**」，則把 y 改為 i 再加-ed；現在分詞則直接加-ing，y 不改變。

cry	cried	cried	crying
study	studied	studied	studying
try	tried	tried	trying

(4)字尾為「**母音＋y**」者，則直接加-ed 及-ing。

| play | played | played | playing |
| enjoy | enjoyed | enjoyed | enjoying |

stay	stayed	stayed	staying

(5)單音節動詞如字尾是單子音而字面是單母音字母(唸起來發所謂短母音)者，要重寫最後子音字母再加-ed 或-ing。

beg	begged	begged	begging
drop	dropped	dropped	dropping
stop	stopped	stopped	stopping
rob	robbed	robbed	robbing

(6)雙音節動詞如重音在第二音節, 而第二音節的結構與(5)相同時, 重寫最後一個子音字母再加-ed 或-ing。

admit	admitted	admitted	admitting
control	controlled	controlled	controlling
permit	permitted	permitted	permitting
prefer	preferred	preferred	preferring
refer	referred	referred	referring

注意: 有些動詞英式英語與美式英語的拚法不同。例如:

travel	(英)	travelled	travelled	travelling
	(美)	traveled	traveled	traveling
worship	(英)	worshipped	worshipped	worshipping
	(美)	worshiped	worshiped	worshiping

《習題 10》

寫出下列動詞的過去式及現在分詞。

1. believe	*believed*	*believing*
2. love	_____	_____
3. come	_____	_____
4. agree	_____	_____
5. lie	_____	_____
6. tie	_____	_____
7. cry	_____	_____
8. study	_____	_____
9. play	_____	_____
10. stay	_____	_____
11. beg	_____	_____
12. prefer	_____	_____
13. stop	_____	_____
14. admit	_____	_____
15. permit	_____	_____
16. travel	_____	_____

第七章
被動語態

7.1. 語態與被動語態(Voice and the Passive Voice)

英語的語態是文法結構方式之一。利用兩種不同的語態——主動與被動——我們可以對句子的動作以兩種不同的方式表達出來,而句子中所描述的事實則不變。試看下面例句:

　　1. Tom hit Peter. (主動語態)湯姆打了彼得。

　　2. Peter was hit by Tom. (被動語態)彼得被湯姆打了。

　　句1與句2所描寫的事實是一樣的, 只是句1比較強調做動作的人(Tom), 而句2則比較強調被動作影響所及的人(Peter)。

7.2. 被動語態的形式(The Formation of the Passive Voice)

　　並不是每一個主動句子都可有相對的被動句。最基本的條件是, 主動句的動詞必須是及物動詞, 才有可能有其對應的被動句。我們可用下面圖解方式表示主動句與被動句的關係:

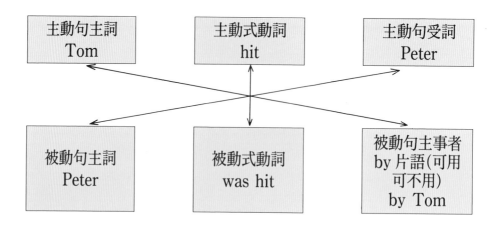

被動句與主動句的動詞形式對應如下表：

(以動詞 take 為例)

時式	主動	被動
簡單現在式	take(s)	$\left\{\begin{array}{l}\text{am}\\\text{are}\\\text{is}\end{array}\right\}$ taken
簡單過去式	took	$\left\{\begin{array}{l}\text{was}\\\text{were}\end{array}\right\}$ taken
簡單將來式	$\left\{\begin{array}{l}\text{will}\\\text{shall}\end{array}\right\}$ take	$\left\{\begin{array}{l}\text{will}\\\text{shall}\end{array}\right\}$ be taken
現在進行式	$\left\{\begin{array}{l}\text{am}\\\text{are}\\\text{is}\end{array}\right\}$ taking	$\left\{\begin{array}{l}\text{am}\\\text{are}\\\text{is}\end{array}\right\}$ being taken
過去進行式	$\left\{\begin{array}{l}\text{was}\\\text{were}\end{array}\right\}$ taking	$\left\{\begin{array}{l}\text{was}\\\text{were}\end{array}\right\}$ being taken

將來進行式	$\left\{\begin{array}{l}\text{will}\\ \text{shall}\end{array}\right\}$ be taking	——
現在完成式	$\left\{\begin{array}{l}\text{have}\\ \text{has}\end{array}\right\}$ taken	$\left\{\begin{array}{l}\text{have}\\ \text{has}\end{array}\right\}$ been taken
過去完成式	had taken	had been taken
將來完成式	$\left\{\begin{array}{l}\text{will}\\ \text{shall}\end{array}\right\}$ have taken	$\left\{\begin{array}{l}\text{will}\\ \text{shall}\end{array}\right\}$ have been taken
現在完成進行式	$\left\{\begin{array}{l}\text{have}\\ \text{has}\end{array}\right\}$ been taking	——
過去完成進行式	had been taking	——
將來完成進行式	$\left\{\begin{array}{l}\text{will}\\ \text{shall}\end{array}\right\}$ have been tak-ing	——

注意：三種完成進行式及將來進行式都沒有列出被動語態, 原因是這幾
　　　種時式極少用被動語態。

有關被動語態, 更多例句列舉如下：

1. This cake *was made* by her mother. 這個蛋糕是她媽媽做
   的。

2. The question will *be answered* by Tom. 這問題將會由
   Tom 回答。

3. He *is* now *being questioned* by the police. 他現在正被警方

查問中。

4. The job **has** just **been done** by her. 這工作剛被她做好了。

5. When we got home, we found that the dishes **had been washed** by Jane. 我們回到家裏時，發現盤子已經被 Jane 洗好了。

6. By next June, the building **will have been completed.** 到明年六月，這幢房子將會已經被建好。

注意： (a)以上例句的中譯有些拗口，因為這些意思在中文通常是用主動句來表達的。

　　　 (b)主動句改成被動句時，動詞與被動句的主詞一致。例如：

　　　 John saw them. John 看見了他們。

　　　 They **were seen** by John. 他們被 John 看見了。

　　　 (c)含有情態助動詞的動詞組，其被動形式比照將來時式的被動式。例如：

　　　 can do → can be done

　　　 would do → would be done

　　　 could give → could be given

　　　 may have done → may have been done 等

7.3. 被動語態的用法

被動語態在英語中最常見的用法有下面幾種：

⑴當我們要強調動作的受事者(亦即主動句中的受詞)時，通常用被動語

態。例如：

1. *He was killed* by a speeding car. 他被一輛超速的汽車撞死。

2. *She was fired* by her boss. 她被她的老闆開除了。

3. *Those books have been sold* by Tom. 那些書被 Tom 賣掉了。

以上三句的重點都在 He、She 及 Those books，亦即動作 killed、fired、sold 的受事者，以及他、她及那些書的遭遇。

(2)當動作的主事者(亦即做動作的人或物)不詳，或是根本不必表示時，通常也用被動語態。例如：

1. She *was told* the good news. 有人告訴她這個好消息。(不知道是誰告訴她這消息的)

2. The streets *are swept* every other day. 街道每隔一天清掃。(清掃街道的人通常是清道夫，因此不必說明)

(3)當主動句中動詞為泛稱或沒有特指的名詞或代名詞(例如，people '人們'、one '人'、someone '某人'、a man '一個人、人'、nobody '沒有人'等)時，通常以被動語態表示，同時也不必使用 by＋NP。例如：

1. a. People *elected* him mayor. 人們選他當市長。

   b. He *was elected* mayor. 他被選為市長。

2. a. One *sees* this sign everywhere. 人們到處都可見到這個標誌。

   b. This sign *is seen* everywhere. 這個標誌到處可見。

3. a. Someone *shut* the door. 有人把門關好。

   b. The door *was shut*. 門關好了。

以上各例句中，b 句要比 a 句更常用，更自然。

⑷少數定型的被動語態片語常用來引導 that 子句，表達不牽涉個人的語氣(例如，it is said '據說'、it is believed '大家都相信'、it is hoped、it is expected '大家／一般都希望／期望'等)。

1. *It is said* that Mr. Wang will resign next month. 據說王先生下個月會辭職。

2. *It was* generally *believed* that Larry was a good mayor. 一般都相信 Larry 是一位好市長。

類似的片語還有: it is assumed '一般都認為'、it is suggested'提議'、it is reported '據報導'等。

7.4.　被動語態使用上的一些限制及應注意事項

7.4.1.　有些動詞只用於主動語態

除了不及物動詞、連繫動詞以外，另外還有一些及物動詞，只能用於主動語態。這類動詞有: have '有'、cost '價值…'、lack '缺少'、hold '容得下'、suit '適合'、resemble '與…相似' 等。例如:

1. I *have* two brothers. 我有兩個弟弟。

2. Richard *resembles* his mother. Richard 長得像他媽媽。

3. They *lack* courage. 他們缺乏勇氣。

4. The hall *holds* 1000 people. 這大堂容得下一千人。

5. This book *cost* two hundred dollars. 這本書價值兩佰元。

以上這些例句都不能說成被動形式。不能說*Two brothers are had by me.或*Courage is lacked by them.等。

7.4.2.　片語動詞

片語動詞如成為一定型而且語意為「及物」的成語時，可用於被動語態。例如：

1. They finally *arrived at* a satifactory conclusion. 他們終於獲得一個令人滿意的結論。(arrive at　'獲得、獲致'為「及物」的片語動詞)

2. They *looked after* the baby very well at home. 他們在家把嬰兒照顧得很好。(look after '照顧'為「及物」的片語動詞，

因此例句1與2可分別寫成：

3. A satisfactory conclusion *was* finally *arrived at.*

4. The baby *was* very well *looked after* at home.

7.4.3.　間接受詞、直接受詞與被動語態

一般說來，動詞如帶間接及直接受詞時，被動句可以有兩種形式。間接受詞與直接受詞都可能做被動句的主詞。例如：

1. I gave *him a book.* 我給他一本書。

句1的被動句可以是：

2. *He* was given a book (by me).

也可以是：

3. *A book* was given (to) him (by me).

通常以主動句中的間接受詞做主詞的被動句比較好, 例如例句 2。另外, 例句 3 中的 to 可以省略。同時, 有些動詞後面不用 to 而用 for 或 of。例如:

　　4. a. She *asked* me a question. 她問我一個問題。

　　　 b. A question *was asked of* me.

　　5. a. I *bought* her a present. 我給她買了一件禮物。

　　　 b. A present *was bought for* her.

此外, 如受詞為反身代名詞, 則不能改為被動句。例如:

　　6. a. John cut *himself* with a knife. John 用小刀割了自己。

　　　 b. *Himself was cut (by John) with a knife.

7.4.4. 被動句中的 by＋主事者片語

在被動句中, 真正做動作的人(亦即動作的主事者)置於 by 後面。但因為被動句經常是強調動作的受事者, 或是主事者不詳、或不重要、或不言而喻, 因此, 被動句的 by＋主事者片語經常省略。

據文法學家 Quirk 等人(1985)所說, 在實際使用時, 英語的被動句每五句當中大約會有四句沒有 by＋主事者片語。因此, 如果被動句沒有 by 片語, 則動作的主事者就不一定, 而也不可能有固定的對應主動句了。例如:

　　1. Joe was hit on the head. Joe 的頭部被打到了。

例句 1 的動作主事者不詳, 我們不知道是誰打了 Joe。所以例句 1 的對應主動句有很多的可能性:

　　2. $\begin{cases} \text{The man} \\ \text{His father} \\ \text{His teacher} \\ \text{Someone} \\ \vdots \end{cases}$ hit Joe on the head.

7.4.5.　get——被動句

被動句的主要助動詞是 be。但是 get 也可以表示被動的語意。例如：

1. She *got beaten* last night. 她昨天晚上挨揍了。
2. The thief *got caught* by the owner of the shop. 小偷給店主人捉到了。
3. The book finally *got translated* into Chinese. 這本書終於被翻譯成中文了。

《習題 11》

(A) 將下列各句改寫爲被動句，並省略 by 片語。

　例：He showed me a picture.

　　　I was given a picture.

1. He hurt his hand.
2. The police asked me a question.
3. They invite all of us to the party.
4. I will write a letter soon.
5. Mr. Smith will send Tom a telegram.
6. By next week I will have paid all the bills.
7. Dr. Johnson will complete the book next month.

(B)將下列各句改寫爲被動句，並省略 by 片語。

1. We should open the door for our teacher.

2. Someone had already washed the dishes when I came into the kitchen.

3. They are blowing up (炸毀) the old bridge.

4. John turned on the light.

5. We must not park our cars here.

6. They will serve orange juice.

7. Why didn't someone fix the radio?

8. You must return the books to the library in two weeks.

9. They have already told Arthur the news.

10. They make sugar at this factory.

11. Someone should tell her to stop crying.

(C)將下列各句改爲被動句, 以間接受詞作被動句的主詞, 省略 by 片語。

　　例：He gave ＿me＿ a book.
　　　　　　　　I.O.

　　I was given a book.

1. He gave me a job in the bank.

2. They sent me a letter.

3. We will buy her a new dress.

4. The waiter handed me a bill.

5. They finally told him the good news.

6. Tom showed me his new picture.

(D)將下列各句改寫爲被動句, 省略 by 片語。

1. They have just put out the fire.

2. He threw out the garbage.

3. That man is mad. People should lock him up.

4. They will never give up the plan.

5. He turned off the gas.

6. The nurse looked after the children properly (正確地).

(E)將下列句子改爲主動句。如原句沒有 by 片語,則提供一個適當的主事者做主動句的
主詞。

例：John was hit by Mary. →

Mary hit John.

I was given a present. →

My father gave me a present.

1. His left eye has just been examined.

2. Your TV set will be fixed.

3. Mary will be given a reward.

4. I was given a cup of tea by Mrs. Kaplan.

5. This machine must have been made by that engineer.

6. The meeting was called off (取消) by the committee yesterday.

7. She was told the good news.

第八章
主要助動詞 Be、Have、Do

8.1. 助動詞概說

8.1.1. 助動詞的種類

　　英語動詞在語意及結構上可以獨立使用的叫「**完整動詞**」或「**普通動詞**」（如 work、see、hit、walk 等），另外有些動詞稱作「**助動詞**」(auxiliary verbs)。這些助動詞主要是與普通動詞連用，以(1)「幫助」普通動詞形成被動式、進行式及完成式；(2)「幫助」普通動詞表達其本身意義以外的一些「情態」（如能力、義務、需要、允許、可能性等）；(3)「幫助」普通動詞形成 yes-no 問句及否定句。

　　助動詞可分為(1)**主要助動詞**(primary auxiliaries) Be、Have、Do 以及(2)**情態助動詞**(modal auxiliaries, 如 can、may、will、could、should、would 等)兩種。

8.1.2. 助動詞的共同特點

助動詞(包括 Be、Have、Do 以及情態助動詞)有以下四種共同特點:

(1)助動詞能與 not 連用, 構成否定句。

1. John *is not* tall. John 不高。
2. Mary *cannot* swim. Mary 不會游泳。
3. She *will not* come here tomorrow. 她明天不會來這裡。
4. I *do not* like him. 我不喜歡他。
5. He *has not* finished doing his homework. 他還沒有做完功課。

注意: 這些助動詞可以與 not 構成略寫/讀形式(contracted form)。例如:

6. John *isn't* tall.
7. Mary *can't* swim.
8. She *won't* come here tomorrow.
9. I *don't* like him.
10. He *hasn't* finished doing his homework.

(2)在形成 yes-no 問句時, 助動詞與主詞要倒裝(易位)。例如:

1. a. *He is* singing. 他正在唱歌。
   b. *Is he* singing? 他正在唱歌嗎?
2. a. *He likes* music. 他喜歡音樂。
   b. *Does he like* music? 他喜歡音樂嗎?
3. a. *He has eaten* his lunch. 他已經吃過午飯。

　b. *Has he eaten* his lunch? 他已經吃過午飯了嗎?

4. a. *He will come* tomorrow. 他明天會來。

　b. *Will he come* tomorrow? 他明天會來嗎?

5. a. *She can speak* English. 她會說英語。

　b. *Can she speak* English? 她會說英語嗎?

(3)助動詞可用於「**附加短問句**」(question　tags)、「**短答句**」(short answers)，或在一些經省略部分單字的結構中，代表前面已說過的完整動詞組。例如:

1. A: You like this dog, *don't* you? A: 你喜歡這隻狗，不是嗎?

　B: $\left\{\begin{array}{l}\text{Yes, I } \textbf{\textit{do}}.\\ \text{No, I } \textbf{\textit{don't}}.\end{array}\right.$ 　B: $\left\{\begin{array}{l}\text{是的，我喜歡。}\\ \text{不，我不喜歡。}\end{array}\right.$

2. I like this dog and so *does* he. 我喜歡這隻狗，他也喜歡。

以上例句中的 do、does、don't 都代表 like 或(does　not　like)　this dog。

(4)除了與 not 形成略寫／讀形式外，be、have、will、would 還可以有以下的略寫／讀式。

　Be: am →'m; is →'s; are →'re

　Have: have →'ve; has →'s; had →'d

　Will: will →'ll

　Would: would →'d

1. I *am* happy. → I*'m* happy. 我很快樂。

2. He *is* happy. → He*'s* happy. 他很快樂。

3. They *are* all here. → They*'re* all here. 他們全都在這兒。

4. I *have* just *eaten* my lunch. → I *'ve* just *eaten* my lunch.
   我剛吃過午飯。

5. She *has* just *gone* to school → She *'s* just *gone* to school.
   她剛上學去。

6. She said she *had made* a cake. → She said she *'d made* a
   cake. 她說她做了一個蛋糕。

7. I *will go* tomorrow. → I *'ll go* tomorrow. 我明天會去。

8. He *would like* to help you. → He *'d like* to help you.
   他願意幫助你。

8.2.　Be

8.2.1.　Be 當助動詞使用

　　除了上面 8.1.2. 所提到, Be 動詞可以與 not 連用形成否定句(如 I *am not* busy), 以及與主詞倒裝形成 yes-no 問句以外(*Is he* busy?), Be 動詞當作助動詞使用時, 還可以有以下的功能:

⑴ Be 與現在分詞(V-ing)連用, 構成進行時式。例如:
　1. He *is doing* his homework. 他正在做功課.
　2. He *was doing* his homework when I went to see him last night. 我昨晚去看他的時候他正在做功課。

⑵ Be 與過去分詞(V-en)連用, 構成被動語態。例如:

1. He **was arrested.** 他被逮捕了。

2. She **is being questioned.** 她正在被詢問。

3. This problem **has not been solved.** 這個問題還沒有解決。

注意：含情態助動詞的句子，其被動句亦以 be 來表示。例如：Some-one **must do** the job. → The job **must be done.**

8.2.2.　Be 當普通動詞使用

⑴ Be 當普通動詞使用時，語意為'是'、'在'等，**具連繫動詞功用，**可以表示職業、身分、情況、精神或身體狀況、年齡、大小、重量、物質、價格等。例如：

1. He **is** a doctor. 他是醫生。

2. Water **is** liquid. 水是液體。

3. Tom **is** in the garden. Tom 在花園裏。

4. She **is** very tall. 她很高。

5. Taiwan **is** an island. 臺灣是個島嶼。

6. I **am** very tired. 我很累。

7. How old **is** she? 她幾歲？

　　She **is** seventeen years old. 她十七歲。

8. How tall **are** you? 你多高？

　　I **am** 170 centimeters. 我身高 170 公分。

9. What **is** you weight? 你有多重？

　　(或 How much do you weigh?)

　　I **am** 55 kilos. 我體重 55 公斤。

10.How much **is** this book? 這本書多少錢？

　　It **'s** 100 dollars. (這本書)一百元。

(2) Be 當普通動詞使用，而其主詞是不定的人或事物時，用「there＋be＋名詞」表示。例如：

1. *There is a man* at the door. 門口有一個人。
2. *There are two students* in the classroom. 教室裡有兩個學生。

注意：1、2 兩句中，眞正的主詞是 a man 與 two students。 There 只是文法上的引導詞，因此，動詞 be 是與眞正的主詞一致。a man 用 is；而 two students 用 are。

8.3.　Have

8.3.1.　Have 當助動詞使用

(1) Have 當助動詞使用，可形成否定句及 yes-no 問句。例如：

1. I *do not have* two brothers. 我沒有兩個弟弟。
2. *Does she have* a sister?　她有沒有妹妹？

(2) Have 當助動詞用，可以構成完成時式。例如：

1. I *have finished* my work. 我已經做完了我的工作。(現在完成式)
2. I *had finished* my homework when you came to see me last night. 昨晚你來看我時，我已經做完功課了。(過去完成式)
3. We *will have lived* here for ten years by next month.

到下個月我們將會在這兒住了十年了。(將來完成式)

8.3.2. Have 當普通動詞使用

⑴當普通動詞使用時，Have 表示「**擁有**」、「**有**」。例如：

1. I *have* some money. 我有一點錢。

2. She *has* a car. 她有一部汽車。

這是 have 的基本意思，以這種意思使用時，have 就如其他普通動詞一樣，否定句及問句的形成都需要助動詞 do。例如：

3. *Do* you *have* any money? 你有錢嗎？

4. I *do not* (*don't*) have any money. 我沒有錢。

注意：⒜在英式英語裏，表示「有」或「擁有」的 have 也可以不用助動詞 do 而形成問句及否定句。例如：

5. *Have* you a car? 你有汽車嗎？

6. I *haven't* any money. 我沒有錢。

但美式英語不用句 5 及 6，而用句 3 及 4 的形式。

⒝動詞若是過去式，即使英式英語也不常用句 5 及 6 的形式。

"Had you any money？" 是相當不自然，也很少聽到的說法。

⑵當普通動詞使用時，have 可表示「**吃／喝**」、「**舉行**」、「**經歷**」、「**遭遇**」等意思。

have 表示這種「動態」的語意時，問句及否定句都需要用助動詞 do 來構成，而且英式與美式英語在這方面並無差異。例如：

1. She usually *has* coffee with her breakfast. 她通常早餐時喝咖啡。

2. We *are having* a party next Saturday. 我們下週六會有(舉行)一個聚會。

3. We *had* a good time last night. 昨天晚上我們玩得很開心。

4. He *is having* lunch now. 他現在正在吃午飯。

5. I *have* breakfast at seven. 我七點鐘吃早餐。

6. *Did* you *have* a good time last night? 你昨天晚上玩得開心嗎?

7. I *didn't have* a good time. 我玩得不開心。

8. *Do* you *have* breakfast at seven? 你早上七點鐘吃早餐嗎?

9. I *did not* take a bath last night. 我昨天晚上沒有洗澡。

注意: 表示「擁有」、「有」時, have 為「靜態」動詞, 不能用進行式。因此我們不能說*I am having a car。但表示「吃／喝」等意思時, have 是「動態」(有動作的)動詞, 可以用進行式。見上面2、4兩例句。

8.4.　Do

8.4.1.　Do 當助動詞使用

⑴句子動詞為簡單現在式或簡單過去式(亦即動詞組本身不帶任何助動詞)時, 其問句及否定句要用 do 來構成。例如:

1. She *wants* to stay. 她想留下來。

2. *Does* she *want* to stay? 她想留下來嗎?

3. She *does not* (*doesn't*) *want* to stay. 她不想留下來。

4. I *promised* to give him a present. 我答應過給他一份禮物。

5. *Did* I *promise* to give him a present? 我答應過給他一份禮物嗎?

6. I *did not promise* to give him a present. 我沒有答應給他一份禮物。

7. I *said* something. 我說了一些話。

8. What *did* I *say*? 我說了些什麼?

9. *Did* I *say* anything? 我說了任何話嗎?

10.I *did not say* anything. 我沒有說過任何話。

⑵肯定句的動詞如是簡單現在式或簡單過去式，要加強語氣時，用 do 或 did，重音唸在 do 或 did 上。例如:

1. I *want* to come. 我想來。

2. I `*do want*` to come. 我真的想來。

3. I *saw* her this morning. 今天早上我看到她。

4. I `*did see*` her this morning. 今天早上我真的看到她。

另外，祈使句也可以加上 Do 來強調，並增加其「說服力」。例如:

5. *Come* in. 請進。

6. *Do come* in! 請進! (語氣更為懇切，說話者更想聽者進來)

⑶do 可以在省略部分語詞的結構中，代表在前面(上文)已經說過的動詞(或述語)。例如:

1. A: Do you like the movie? 你喜歡這電影嗎?

   B: Yes, I *do.* 喜歡。(do＝"like the movie")

2. A: Did he stay? 他有沒有留下來?

   B: Yes, he *did.* 有，他留下來了。(did＝"stay")

或 No, he ***didn't.*** 沒有, 他沒有留下來。(didn't＝"did not stay")

3. She runs faster than I ***do.*** 她跑得比我快。(do＝"run")

4. I don't like swimming but she ***does.*** 我不喜歡游泳, 但她却喜歡。(does＝"like swimming")

這種用法也適用於附加短問句(tag questions)。例如:

5. He didn't arrive on time, ***did*** he? 他沒有準時到達, 是嗎? (did＝"arrive on time")

8.4.2.　Do 當普通動詞使用

當普通動詞使用時, do 基本的意思是「**做**」、「**從事**」、「**進行**」等。問句及否定句都要用助動詞 do 來構成。例如:

1. He usually ***does*** his homework in the evening. 他通常在晚上做功課。

2. ***Does*** he usually ***do*** his homework in the evening? 他通常在晚上做功課嗎?

3. He ***does not*** (***doesn't***) usually do his homework in the evening. 他通常不在晚上做功課。

4. What ***is*** he ***doing*** now? 他現在做什麼?

5. What ***does*** he ***do*** for a living? 他做什麼來維持生活?

6. How ***are*** you ***doing***? (do＝get on) 你這一向可好?

7. I ***didn't do*** my job well. 我沒有把我的工作做好。

8. She ***is not doing*** very well at school. 她在學校表現得不很好。(功課並不很好)

《習題 12》

(A)填入 have 的適當形式。

　例：We *are having* dinner now.

　　　We *had* a party yesterday.

　　　Has he *finished* his work?

1. Come in!　We _____an interesting discussion right now.

2. Why were they late?

　They _____a flat tire.

3. We _____a party next Sunday.

4. Let's not disturb (打擾) our teacher. He _____a rest.

5. What _____ you _____for dinner?

　I _____ roast beef and green salad.

6. Did you enjoy yourself last night?

　Oh, yes. I _____a wonderful time.

7. Why didn't you talk to her?

　Well, I _____(not have) a chance.

8. _____you been here before?

9. We _____dinner with him tomorrow night.

10. That was the only thing we could do at that time. We _____no choice.

(B) 填入動詞 be 的正確形式。

　例：(a) He _____making a cake now.

　　　He is making a cake now.

　　　(b) He _____given a book yesterday.

He was given a book yesterday.

1. It ＿＿＿＿＿ not easy to drive along this highway.

2. I ＿＿＿＿＿ here tomorrow.

3. When I saw him last night, he ＿＿＿＿＿ very happy.

4. Jean ＿＿＿＿＿ learning Japanese right now.

5. A: How do you feel about his carelessness?

　　B: I ＿＿＿＿＿ very angry about it.

(C)將下列各句改寫成問句，使用助動詞 do。

　　例：He wrote a book last year.

　　　　Did he write a book last year?

1. I sent him a letter last week.

2. Tom showed me his new shirt.

3. I want to get better grades (分數).

4. She called on (探訪) her uncle last Saturday.

5. Nelson has the key to the house.

6. She obeys her parents.

7. He gave her the correct answer.

8. He cooks his own meals.

9. He drinks lemon juice.

10. Robin's car broke down yesterday.

第九章
情態助動詞

9.1. 情態助動詞的特性

　　情態助動詞(Modal Auxiliaries)包括 *can*、*could*、*may*、*might*、*shall*、*should*、*will*、*would*、*must*、*dare*、*need*、*ought to*、*used to* 等。這些助動詞除了「幫助」普通動詞構成問句及否定句，還表示動詞本意以外的某些「情態」(例如可能性、能力、義務、意願等)。此外，情態助動詞還具有以下文法結構及用法上的特徵：

　　1.情態助動詞後面接動詞原形：
　　　例如：can ***do***、may ***do***、will ***do***、will ***have*** 等。
　　2.情態助動詞沒有不定詞或分詞的形式：
　　　例如：*to may、*maying、*mayed 等形式是不合文法的。
　　3.情態助動詞沒有第三人稱單數現在式的-s 字尾：
　　　例如：He can do it.不可說成*He cans do it.

9.2. 情態助動詞的用法

情態助動詞大致可分為最常用的「**主要情態助動詞**」(包括 *can*、*could*、*may*、*might*、*shall*、*should*、*will*、*would*、*must*)，以及「**次要情態助動詞**」(包括 *ought to*、*used to* 等)兩種。

9.2.1. Can／Could

否定式：cannot、can't／could not、couldn't

⑴ can 可表示「**能力**」。
　1. *Can* you *help* me? 你能幫我忙嗎?
　2. He *can move* this heavy table. 他能移動這張重的桌子。
　3. I *can speak* English. 我會說英語。

⑵ can 可表示「**可能性**」。
　1. The rain *can stop* in a few hours. 雨可能在幾小時之內會停。
　2. There *can be* a party next Tuesday. 下星期二可能會有一次聚會。

⑶ can 可用來**請求許可**或表示**許可**。例如:
　1. *Can* I *come* in? 我可以進來嗎?
　2. You *can leave* now. 你現在可以走了。

注意：cannot 可表示「禁止」之意。例如：

You cannot park your car here.　（你不可把車子停在此地。）

⑷ could 可以表示請求允許，語氣比 can 更委婉及更有禮貌。例如：

1. *Could* I *come* in?　我可以進來嗎？

2. *Could* I *speak* in Chinese?　我可以用中文說嗎？

⑸ could 可以表示過去的允許、能力等。通常與另一個過去式動詞或表示過去時間的語詞連用。例如：

1. She *said* I *could leave.*　她說我可以走。

2. I *couldn't find* my book yesterday.　昨天我找不到我的書。

9.2.2.　May ／ Might

否定式：　may not、mayn't ／ might not、mightn't

⑴ may 與 might 表示「**可能性**」。例如：

1. It *may ／ might rain* today.　今天可能會下雨。

2. I *may ／ might go* to Tainan tomorrow.　我明天可能到臺南去。

⑵ may 可表示**允許、許可**。例如：

1. You *may come* in.　你可以進來。

2. I *may go* home in a few minutes.　幾分鐘之後我就可以回家了。

3. *May* I *use* your telephone?　我可以用你的電話嗎？

Yes, you *may*.　可以。

No, you *may not*.　不可以。

　　請求允許時, 如例句3, 也可用 might, 語氣比較更禮貌。另外, 在比較不正式的場合及用法中, 以上各例句中 may 與 can 都可通用。

　　(3)如句子的主要動詞或條件子句中的動詞是過去式時, 要用 might。例如:

1. He *said* that I *might use* his telephone.　他說我可以用他的電話。
2. If you *woke* the baby up, it *might cry*.　如果你把那嬰兒吵醒, 他可能會哭。

9.2.3.　Shall ╱ Should

　　否定式: shall not、shan't ╱ should not、shouldn't

9.2.3.1.　shall

　　⑴從文法上說, shall 可表示第一人稱將來式, 但在美式英語中, 已經被 will 所取代。即使在英式英語裏, 口語中也愈來愈少人用 shall 來表示將來式。因此, 類似 I *will ╱ shall* go tomorrow.的句子, 通常是用 will 為主。

　　⑵shall 用於 let's 後面之附加短問句, 以及表示提議、請求命令或指示的問句中。例如:

1. Let's go home, *shall* we?　我們回家去吧, 好嗎?
2. *Shall* we go by bus?　我們坐公車去好嗎? (提議)

3. *Shall* I do my homework here?　我要不要就在這兒做功課呢?（請求指示）

⑶ shall 可表示決心。

在平常表示決心用 will，但在特別強調時（如演說），可以用 shall 來表示決心。例如:

I *shall* return.　我一定會回來的。

9.2.3.2.　should

⑴ should 表示**義務／責任**。

1. You *should hand in* your homework right now.　你應該現在把功課交來。

2. We *should pay* our rent on the first day of each month.　我們應該在每月第一天交房租。

⑵在**間接**（引述／報導）**句式中**，或在其他**複合句子**裏，should **與過去式動詞連用，表示義務／責任，或推斷**。例如:

1. He *said* to me that I *should study* hard.　他對我說我應該用功唸書。（義務）

2. I thought he *should be* on time.　我認爲他應該準時的。（推斷；因爲他一向都準時）

注意: 按現在的情況或事實所作的推斷也可用 should。

如: Tom is a good friend of Mary's.　So, he *should know* her name.　Tom 是 Mary 的好朋友。因此，他應該知道她的名字。

9.2.4.　Will ／ Would

否定式：will not、won't ／ would not、wouldn't

9.2.4.1.　will

⑴ will 構成**簡單將來時式,** 表示將來的語意。

　　1. She *will be* seventeen next month.　下個月她就十七歲了。

　　2. I *will call* you tomorrow.　我明天會打電話給你。

⑵ will 可以表示**各種不同強度的意志,** 例如打算、意願、允諾、決心等。

　　1. We *will write* you soon.　我們很快就會寫信給你。(打算)

　　2. I *will help* you.　我會幫助你的。(意願)

　　3. If you come on time, I *will teach* you how to type.　如果你準時來到的話, 我就教你打字。(允諾)

　　4. We *will* certainly *work* hard.　我們一定會努力工作。(決心)

⑶ will 可以表示**推測。**

　　1. You *will feel* better after you eat something.　吃點東西以後你會覺得舒服些。(將來的推測)

　　2. Let's give him a call, he *'ll be* at home now.　我們打電話給他吧, 他現在會在家的。(現在的推測)

　　3. Oil *will float* on water.　油會浮在水面上。(習慣的推測)

⑷ will 與 you 連用可以表示**請求。**例如:

　　1. *Will* you *sit* down?　你可以坐下來嗎?

2. *Will* you *open* the door, please?　請你把門打開好嗎？

9.2.4.2.　would

⑴ would 為 will 的過去形式，可表示 will 的各種用法。例如：

1. He said I *would feel* better after I ate something.　他說我吃點東西以後就會覺得舒服些。(推測)

2. She said that she *would call* me.　她說她會打電話給我。(打算)

3. John told me that he *would study* hard because he wanted to pass the exam.　John 告訴我說他一定會用功唸書，因為他想考試及格。(決心)

4. When he was in high school, he *would go* jogging every morning.　他唸中學時每天早上都會去慢跑。(過去習慣)

⑵ would 表示請求時，語氣比 will 更客氣及禮貌。例如：

1. *Would* you *open* the door, please?　請你開門好嗎？

2. *Would* you please *come* in?　請進來。

⑶ would rather (sooner) than 表示「偏好」、「寧可」之意。例如：

1. I *would rather* play basketball *than* tennis.　我寧可打籃球而不打網球。

2. He *would rather* go to the movies *than* stay home.　他寧可去看電影而不願留在家裏。

9.2.5.　Must

否定式：must not、mustn't

⑴ must 表示**義務、責任、需要或加強語氣的勸告**。

1. We *must pay* our bill now.　我們現在必須付賬。
2. A driver *must drive* carefully.　司機必須小心開車。
3. You *must come* tomorrow night.　明天晚上你一定要來。
4. You *must work* harder next time.　下次你必須更用功一點。
 （勸告）

⑵ must 可表示**推斷。特別是有明顯的理由所支持的推斷**。例如：

Mary：I've been working for ten hours.

Tom：You *must be* very tired.

Mary：我一直不斷地工作了十個鐘頭。

Tom：那你一定很累了。

⑶ must not 表示**禁止、不許**。因此，You must go. 的意思是「你必須去」，但 You must not go. 卻表示「你不可以去」(而不是*「你不必去」)。例如：

You *must not smoke* here.　你不可以在這裏抽煙。

注意：如要表示「不必、不需要」，用 need not 或 do／does not have to。例如：

I *must go.* 我必須去。

I *need not go.* 我不必去。

I *don't have to go.* 我不必去。

9.2.6. 次要情態助動詞

9.2.6.1. ought to

否定式：ought not、oughtn't

ought to 的用法大多數與 should 相似。例如：

1. You *ought to be* here on time. 你應該準時到這裏。(義務、責任)
2. You *ought to stop* (*quit*) smoking. 你應該戒煙。(勸告)
3. He's been studying very hard. He *ought to pass* the exam. 他一直很用功唸書，(所以)他考試應該及格的。(推斷)

9.2.6.2. used to

used to 主要表示**過去的習慣或過去例行的動作**。例如：

1. I *used to drink* tea; now I drink coffee.
   我以往喝茶；現在喝咖啡。
2. When he was in college, he *used to stay* up late. 他在大學時，常常很晚才睡。

《習題 13》

⒜將下列各句改為否定句。

例：I can swim. →

    I cannot (can't) swim.

    I want to swim.　→

    I do not (don't) want to swim.

1. We have to go home.

2. He is ten years old.

3. She saw John yesterday.

4. They can speak English.

5. I will wait for you.

6. Alice should leave now.

7. She ought to have tea.

8. She may stay here.

9. You were wrong.

10. Joan had a headache.

11. You must tell him the truth.

12. You may come in.

(B)將下列各句改爲問句。

    例：He can swim.　→

        Can he swim?

        He wants to swim.　→

        Does he want to swim?

1. You drink beer.

2. I had some toast for breakfast this morning.

3. This is a personal computer.

4. He may borrow my car.

5. We will have a party tomorrow.

6. I must do it at once.

7. She can leave it here.

8. John should try again.

9. He will buy a Sony Walkman.

10. You did it well.

(C)在以下空格中，填入 can 或 could。

1. A: Can you do 30 push-ups (伏地挺身) in a minute?

   B: I_____when I was in the army, but I_____(not) now.

2. When I first went to the U.S., I_____(not) say anything in English.
   But now I_____speak it very well.

3. A: How fast_____you run?

   B: I_____run very fast.

4. He told me that he_____(not) see anything at that time.

5. When I was a child, I_____sing very well.

(D)填入 may 或 might。

1. A: _____I come in.

   B: Sure. Please do.

2. _____I borrow your typewriter?

3. She said she_____win the game.

4. It_____rain. You had better take an umbrella with you.

5. You_____stay here for a short time.

6. He_____never come again.

7. He told me that he_____be late.

(E)填入 would 或 should。

1. _____you help me with this exercise please?

2. We_____help the poor people.

3. He_____rather come here than stay at home.

4. I think he_____tell her what to do.

5. Tom has been living here for ten years, he_____know where the post-office is. ˙

6. She said she_____be home early.

7. What_____you like? Tea or coffee?

第十章
問句的形成

10.1. 詞序及問句的種類

英語問句形成過程中，常涉及詞序的改變，特別是主詞及動詞的「倒裝」(即主詞與動詞順序調換)。因此，詞序是問句形成的一個重要因素。

英語問句主要有「Yes-No 問句」及「Wh-問句」(又稱為「疑問詞問句」)兩種。另外，句末的附加短問句也是日常使用之問句形式之一。

以下分別討論這三種問句的構形，以及其用法。

10.2. Yes-No 問句

「Yes-No」問句的名稱是因為這種問句可以用 Yes 或 No 來回答而得來。Yes-No 問句主要由主詞動詞倒裝而形成。可分下列三種。

10.2.1.　含 be 動詞的句子

含 be 動詞的句子，以 be 與主詞倒裝構成 Yes-No 問句。

主詞＋be…→ Be＋主詞…?

例如:

1. *He is* a student.　他是學生。
 Is he a student?　他是學生嗎?
 答句是: Yes, he is.或 No, he isn't.
2. *They are* your classmates.　他們是你的同學。
 Are they your classmates?　他們是你的同學嗎?
 答句是: Yes, they are.或 No, they　aren't.
3. *She was* late for class.　她上課遲到。
 Was she late for class?　她上課遲到了嗎?
 答句是: Yes, she was.或 No, she wasn't.

10.2.2.　含有助動詞的句子

含有助動詞的句子，以助動詞與主詞倒裝構成 Yes-No 問句:

主詞＋助動詞＋V…→助動詞＋主詞＋V…?

例如:

1. *He can* swim.　他會游泳。
 Can he swim?　他會游泳嗎?

答句：Yes, he can.或 No, he can't.

2. ***She will*** be fifteen next month.　她下個月就十五歲了。

Will she be fifteen next month?　她是不是下個月就十五歲了？

答句：Yes, she will.或 No, she won't.

3. ***They are*** dancing.　他們正在跳舞。

Are they dancing?　他們正在跳舞嗎？

答句：Yes, they are.或 No, they aren't.

4. ***He was*** tired.　他累了。

Was he tired?　他累了嗎？

答句：Yes, he was.或 No, he wasn't.

5. ***She has*** arrived.　她已經到了。

Has she arrived?　她已經到了嗎？

答句：Yes, she has.或 No, she hasn't.

6. ***He may*** go now.　他現在可以走了。

May he go now?　他現在可以走了嗎？

答句：Yes, he may.或 No, he may not.

10.2.3.　不帶 be 動詞或任何助動詞的句子

如句子只不含 be 動詞或任何助動詞時, 我們需要加入助動詞 do, 才能構成 Yes-No 問句, do 的人稱及數必須與主詞一致。

$$
\text{主詞} + \begin{Bmatrix} \text{V} \\ \text{V-(es)} \\ \text{V-ed} \end{Bmatrix} \cdots \rightarrow \begin{Bmatrix} \text{Do} \\ \text{Does} \\ \text{Did} \end{Bmatrix} + \text{主詞} + \text{V} \cdots ?
$$

例如：

1. You *like* swimming.　你喜歡游泳。

   Do you *like* swimming?　你喜歡游泳嗎？

   答句：Yes, I do.或 No, I don't.

2. He *saw* Mary yesterday.　他昨天看見 Mary。

   Did he *see* Mary yesterday?　他昨天看見 Mary 了嗎？

   答句：Yes, he did. 或 No, he didn't.

3. She *likes* fast food.　她喜歡速食。

   Does she *like* fast food?　她喜歡速食嗎？

   答句：Yes, she does.或 No, she doesn't.

4. They *have* two brothers.　他們有兩個兄弟。

   Do they *have* two brothers?　他們有兩個兄弟嗎？

   答句：Yes, they do.或 No, they don't.

10.2.4.　Yes-No 問句與語調

Yes-No **問句通常以上升語調**(rising intonation)**說出來**。例如：

1. Is he a student?　↗ 他是個學生嗎？

2. Did he see Mary yesterday?　↗ 他昨天看見了 Mary 嗎？

3. Will you go there? ↗ 你會到那兒嗎？

4. Has he done anything wrong? ↗ 他做錯了什麼事嗎？

Yes-No 問句的**答句則用一般陳述句的下降語調**(falling　intonation)。例如：

5. Yes, he is. ↘ 或 No, he isn't.↘

6. Yes, he did. ↘ 或 No, he didn't.↘

注意: 有時候, 一個普通句子, 如以上升語調說出來, 也可以成爲 Yes-No 問句。例如:

　　7. You have the key? ↗ 你有鑰匙嗎?

　　　 No, I don't. ↘ 我沒有。

10.3.　Wh-問句

Wh-問句又稱爲「**疑問詞問句**」。這些問句含有疑問詞 *what* '什麼'、*who* '誰'、*whom* '誰' (受格)、*when* '何時'、*where* '何處'、*why* '爲何'、*which* '哪一個'、*how* '如何' 等。

Yes-No 問句通常是問該句所述是否眞實, 因此答句說出「是」'Yes' 或「否」'No' 就足夠。

但 Wh-問句則是對句子的主詞、受詞, 或動作有所不知, 因此答話者必須針對疑問所在(如 '誰'、'何時'、'爲何' 等), 提供確切的資訊, 方能回答問題。

一般說來, 我們可以依疑問詞取代之語詞分爲六種 Wh-問句的主要句型。

取代之語詞	Wh-語詞
1. 主詞	*who*、*what*、*which*
2. 受詞	*who* / *whom*、*what*、*which*
3. 時間副詞	*when*
4. 地方副詞	*where*
5. 原因副詞	*why*
6. 狀態副詞	*how*

10.3.1.　疑問詞為主詞

原句　　　　Wh-問句

$$主詞+V\cdots\rightarrow \begin{Bmatrix} \text{Who} \\ \text{What} \\ \text{Which} \end{Bmatrix}+V\cdots?$$

主詞與動詞不倒裝。

1. *Someone* told Mary the truth.　有人把真相告訴 Mary。
   Who told Mary the truth?　誰把真相告訴 Mary?
2. *Something* happened.　某事發生了。
   What happened?　發生了什麼事?
3. *Either A or B* is a good choice.　A 或 B 都是好的選擇。
   Which is a good choice?　哪一個才是好的選擇?

10.3.2.　疑問詞為受詞

原句　　　　　　　　　　　　Wh-問句

$$主詞+\begin{Bmatrix} \text{V} \\ \text{Aux}+\text{V} \end{Bmatrix}+受詞\cdots\rightarrow \begin{Bmatrix} \text{Who} \\ \text{What} \\ \text{Which} \end{Bmatrix}+\begin{Bmatrix} \text{do} \\ \text{Aux} \end{Bmatrix}+$$

$$主詞+\begin{Bmatrix} \text{V} \\ \text{V} \end{Bmatrix}\cdots?$$

主詞與動詞要倒裝。例如:

1. Nancy made *a cake.* Nancy 做了一個蛋糕。

    → *What did* Nancy *make*? Nancy 做了什麼?

2. They will visit *their uncle* next month. 他們下個月會探望他們的叔叔。

    → *Who(m) will* they *visit* next month? 他們下個月會探望誰?

3. You like *either A or B*. 你喜歡 A 或 B。

    → *Which do* you *like*? 你喜歡哪一個?

注意: 當受詞使用時, 除正式文體外, whom 很少使用。大多數情形都使用 who。但在介詞後面則只能用 whom。例如, For whom did Nancy make this cake? (但這種句式非常正式, 在口語中極少使用, 口語會說 Who did Nancy make this cake for?)

10.3.3. 疑問詞為時間副詞

原句　　　　　　　　　　　　　**Wh-問句**

$$
\text{主詞} + \begin{cases} \text{be} \cdots \\ \text{Aux} + \text{V} \cdots \\ \text{V} \cdots \end{cases} + \text{時間副詞} \rightarrow \text{When} \begin{cases} \text{be} \\ \text{Aux} \\ \text{do} \end{cases} +
$$

$$
\text{主詞} + \begin{cases} \cdots \\ \text{V} \cdots \\ \text{V} \cdots \end{cases} ?
$$

主詞與動詞要倒裝。例如:

1. She was tired *yesterday*. 她昨天很累。

   → *When was she* tired? 她什麼時候很累?

2. He will go to Hong Kong *next week*. 他下星期會去香港。

   → *When will he go* to Hong Kong? 他什麼時候會去香港?

3. They bought the book *two days ago*. 他們兩天前買了這本書。

   → *When did they buy* the book? 他們什麼時候買了這本書?

10.3.4. 疑問詞為地方副詞

原句　　　　　　　　　　　　Wh-問句

$$
主詞 + \left\{ \begin{array}{l} be\cdots \\ Aux+V\cdots \\ V\cdots \end{array} \right\} + 地方副詞 \rightarrow Where + \left\{ \begin{array}{l} be \\ Aux \\ do \end{array} \right\} +
$$

$$
主詞 + \left\{ \begin{array}{l} \cdots \\ V\cdots \\ V\cdots \end{array} \right\} ?
$$

主詞與動詞要倒裝。例如:

1. John was *in Los Angeles* last week. 上星期 John 在洛杉磯。

   → *Where* was John last week? 上星期 John 在哪裏?

2. We can park our car *here*.　我們可以在這兒停車。

　　→ *Where* can we park our car?　我們可以把車子停在哪裏?

3. She put the book *on the shelf*.　她把書放在架子上。

　　→ *Where* did she put the book?　她把書放在哪兒?

4. He has put his pen *in the drawer*.　他已經把筆放在抽屜裏。

　　→ *Where* has he put his pen?　他已經把筆放在哪兒?

10.3.5.　疑問詞爲原因副詞

原句　　　　　　　　　　Wh-問句

$$主詞 + \begin{Bmatrix} be\cdots \\ Aux+V\cdots \\ V\cdots \end{Bmatrix} + 原因副詞 → Why + \begin{Bmatrix} be \\ Aux \\ do \end{Bmatrix} + 主詞 + \begin{Bmatrix} \cdots \\ V\cdots \\ V\cdots \end{Bmatrix} ?$$

主詞與動詞要倒裝。例如:

1. He was late *for some reason*.　他因爲某種理由而遲到。

　　→ *Why* was he late?　他爲什麼遲到?

2. The bank will close *for security reason*.　這銀行將會因安全的理由而關閉。

　　→ *Why* will the bank close?　這銀行爲什麼要關閉?

3. She likes that doll *because* it looks lovely.　她喜歡那個洋娃娃, 因爲它看起來很可愛。

　　→ *Why* does she like that doll?　她爲什麼喜歡那個洋娃娃?

10.3.6.　疑問詞為狀態副詞

原句　　　　　　　　　　　　Wh-問句

$$主詞 + \left\{ \begin{array}{l} Aux+V\cdots \\ V\cdots \end{array} \right\} + 狀態副詞 \rightarrow How + \left\{ \begin{array}{l} Aux \\ do \end{array} \right\} +$$

$$主詞 + \left\{ \begin{array}{l} V\cdots \\ V\cdots \end{array} \right\} ?$$

主詞與動詞要倒裝。例如:

1. She sings *very well*.　她唱歌唱得很好。

   → *How* does she sing?　她唱歌唱得怎樣?

2. They will leave the city *secretly*.　他們將會秘密地離開這個城市。

   → *How* will they leave this city?　他們會怎樣離開這個城市?

10.3.7.　疑問詞的一些其他用法

(1) What 與 Which 可以置於名詞之前(具形容詞功能), 構成 Wh-問句。例如:

1. *What time* do we have our English class?　我們什麼時候(幾點鐘)上英文課?

2. *What day* is today?　今天星期幾?

3. *What age* are you?　你今年幾歲?

4. **Which student** do you like better?　你比較喜歡哪個學生?

(2) Whose 可以取代所有格語詞, 構成 Wh-問句。

1. This is **John's book**.　這是 John 的書。

　→ **Whose** book is this?　這是誰的書?

2. **Tom's car** broke down.　Tom 的車子壞了。

　→ **Whose** car broke down?　誰的車子壞了?

3. You borrowed **Mary's** typewriter.　你借了 Mary 的打字機。

　→ **Whose** typewriter did you borrow?　你借了誰的打字機?

(3) how 可以與 old、deep、high、tall、long、wide、many、much 等字連用, 構成詢問年齡、深度、高度、長度、數量、次數等的 Wh-問句。例如:

1. **How many** students do you have?　你有多少個學生?

2. **How old** are you?　你幾歲?

3. **How deep** is this river?　這條河有多深?

4. **How high** is the mountain?　這座山有多高?

5. **How long** is the rope?　這條繩索有多長?

6. **How tall** is Larry?　Larry 有多高?

7. **How wide** is this desk?　這張桌子有多寬?

另外, how 也可以與其他形容詞或副詞連用, 構成 Wh-問句。例如:

8. **How important** is this lesson?　這一課有多重要?

9. **How fast** can she run?　她能夠跑多快?

10.4. 附加短問句(Tag Questions)

附加短問句是在陳述句後面附加短句，形式為問句。問話者通常期望答話者同意或證實他在陳述句子中所說的話。

10.4.1. 附加短問句的結構

(1)原陳述句　　　　　　　　　　**附加短問句**

　*a.*主詞＋be…,　　　　　　be＋not＋主詞(代名詞)？

　*b.*主詞＋not＋be…,　　　　be＋主詞(代名詞)？

例如:

1. *He is* tired, *isn't he*?　他累了，不是嗎？

2. *John isn't (is not)* tired,　*is he*?　John 不累，對嗎？

3. *They are* sailors, *aren't they*?　他們是水手，不是嗎？

4. *They aren't* sailors, *are they*?　他們不是水手，對嗎？

(2)原陳述句　　　　　　　　　　　**附加短問句**

　*a.*主詞＋助動詞＋動詞…,　　　助動詞＋not＋主詞(代名詞)？

　*b.*主詞＋助動詞＋not＋動詞…,　助動詞＋主詞(代名詞)？

例如:

1. *Peter will* come, *won't he*?　Peter 會來的，不是嗎？

2. *John won't* come, *will he*?　John 不會來的，對嗎？

3. *He can* swim, *can't he*?　他會游泳，不是嗎？

4. *He can't* swim, *can he*?　他不會游泳，對嗎？

(3)**原陳述句**　　　　　　　　　　**附加短問句**

　　*a.*主詞＋動詞…,　　　　　　do＋not＋主詞(代名詞)?

　　*b.*主詞＋do＋not＋動詞…,　do＋主詞(代名詞)?

例如：

1. *She smokes*, *doesn't she*?　她抽煙，不是嗎?

2. *She doesn't smoke, does she?*　她不抽煙，對嗎?

3. *They like* to study English, *don't they?*　他們喜歡唸英文，不是嗎?

4. *They don't like* to study English, *do they?*　他們不喜歡唸英文，對嗎?

10.4.2.　附加短問句其他注意事項

⑴附加短問句中如不用略寫(讀)式 *n't*(如 isn't、aren't 等)時, *not* 應置於句末。例如：

1. He is tired, *is he not?*

2. She will come, *will she not?*

注意: 此種用法很正式，口語中通常用 *n't* 形式。

⑵注意以下特別的助動詞用法。

1. Let's go, *shall we*?　我們走吧，好嗎?

2. Let's not go, *all right*? (或 *O.K.*?)　我們不要去，好嗎?

3. Come in, *will you*?　進來，好嗎?

4. Don't go out, *will you*?　不要走出去，好嗎?

　(3)附加短問句的問話者通常期望答話者同意或證實他在陳述句部分所說的話，但有這種期望時，通常問話者會以「下降語調」說出來。如以「上升語調」說出時，這種期望就相當弱，全句就變得與一句普通的 Yes-No 問句差不多。

《習題 14》

(A)將下列各句改成問句。

　1. She is here.

　2. He studied electrical engineering（電機工程）.

　3. We must work hard.

　4. I had to wash the dishes first.

　5. You want to help John.

　6. A passenger（旅客）just came in.

　7. The plane took off a few minutes ago.

　8. This umbrella belongs to him.

　9. He is a good teacher.

10. She speaks Hebrew（希伯來語）.

11. Betty can open the jar.

12. I will have to hurry.

13. I could go there last night.

14. She heard the bell ringing.

15. Alice felt comfortable.

(B)以短答句來回答下列問句。

　例： Can you swim?

Yes, I can.或 No, I can't.

Does she live here?

Yes, she does.或 No, she doesn't.

1. Is she rich?

2. Can you speak French?

3. Has she done her homework?

4. Is it safe to cross the street here?

5. Is there a book on the desk?

6. Do we have to eat this?

7. Is she coming back on Sunday?

8. Could she be our new teacher?

9. Did he say anything?

10. Are you afraid of mice (老鼠)?

11. Would you like to say something?

12. Does Tom have a car?

(C)用 Who, What 或 Which 來取代句子中之 someone, something 或 either A or B, 構成 Wh-問句。

例：Someone came.

→ Who came?

I saw someone.

→ Who(m) did I see?

1. Something happened.

2. Someone doesn't like Mary.

3. Something seems strange.

4. Someone lives in that house.

5. Either this pen or that pen is lost.

6. Someone wants to see you.

7. She met someone yesterday.

8. He is interested in something.

9. This word means something.

10. You like either tea or coffee.

(D)用 When 取代時間副詞結構，形成問句。

　　例：Tom came yesterday.

　　　　→ When did Tom come?

1. They had English classes this morning.

2. She will have her birthday party tomorrow.

3. They held a meeting (開會) yesterday.

4. They visited their uncle last week.

5. Alice went downtown (到城中鬧區) this morning.

6. They built a house last summer.

7. He bought a T-shirt last Monday.

8. She will come back next month.

9. We have a lot of rain here in May.

10. We saw Thomas last night.

(E)以 Where 取代地方副詞結構，形成問句。

　　例：Mary stays in her room.

　　　　→ Where does Mary stay?

1. John is singing in the bathroom.

2. She keeps her Walkman (隨身聽) in her drawer.

3. Tom was working in the office when you called.

4. Mary was in the kitchen.

5. Tom bought this shirt at the department store.

6. He is going to have a birthday party at a restaurant.

7. She sent her son to school.

8. John goes to church every Sunday morning.

9. He put the money in the safe（保險箱）.

10. Tom will go to Japan next Monday.

(F)以 Why 取代原因／理由副詞結構，形成問句。

　例：He failed because he was lazy.

　　→ Why did he fail?

1. She came here in order to study.

2. Tom was angry because Mary was absent（缺席）.

3. He broke the glass because he was careless.

4. They were happy because they heard the good news.

5. Nancy went to the store for some sugar.

6. Father gave me a bicycle for my birthday.

7. He was punished for not handing in his homework on time.

8. I went to the post office to buy some stamps.

(G)以 How 取代狀態副詞結構，形成問句。

　例：He ran very fast.

　　→ How did he run?

1. Steve worked very hard.

2. She washed her silk dress carefully.

3. Joan sings beautifully.

4. The doctor examined the patient thoroughly（徹底地）.

5. He answered the question correctly.

6. She talked loudly.

7. Our product (產品) sells well.

8. He wrote the letter with pencil.

(H)填入適當的附加短問句。

　例：She likes him, *doesn't she*?

　　　→ She doesn't like him, *does she*?

1. I don't want to do this, _____?

2. She likes to study physics (物理), _____?

3. Larry studies French (法文), _____?

4. You lost the key, _____?

5. You should help him, _____?

6. I can't leave right now, _____?

7. We haven't seen Tom lately (最近), _____?

8. They will arrive on time, _____?

9. She was hit on the head, _____?

10. He wasn't nervous, _____?

11. I am a student, _____?

12. Let's help her, _____?

13. Don't come in, _____?

14. She never sings in class, _____?

15. Sit down, _____?

16. Let's not go out in the rain, _____?

第十一章
否定句的形成

　　英語的否定句主要以 not 與動詞連用而形成；除此之外，有些否定語詞與用語也可以用來構成否定句，分別描述如下。

11.1.　Not＋動詞

11.1.1.　含 be 動詞的句子

肯定句	否定句

主詞＋be…→主詞＋be＋not…

例如:

1. He *is* happy.
   他快樂。
   He *is not* happy.
   他不快樂。

2. She *was* in the kitchen.　她在廚房裏。

She *was not* in the kitchen.　她不在廚房裏。

3. We *are* here.　我們在這兒。

We *are not* here.　我們不在這兒。

4. They *were* tired.　他們累了。

They *were not* tired.　他們不累。

Be 與 not 常可略寫(讀)成 isn't、wasn't、aren't、weren't。

另外，is not及are not、am not也可略寫(讀)為's not、're not, 及 'm not。例如:

5. He *isn't* here.　他不在這兒。

He *'s not* here.

6. We *aren't* students.　我們不是學生。

We *'re not* students.

7. I *am not* a scientist.　我不是一個科學家。

I *'m* not a scientist.

11.1.2.　含助動詞的句子

肯定句　　　　　否定句

主詞＋助動詞＋動詞…→主詞＋助動詞＋not＋動詞…

例如:

1. He *is singing*.　他正在唱歌。

He *is not singing*.　他不是在唱歌。

2. I *have done* my homework.　我已經做完功課。

　　I *have not done* my homework.　我還沒做完功課。

3. She *can speak* English.　她會說英語。

　　She *cannot speak* English.　她不會說英語。

助動詞與 not 常可略寫(讀)：

　　have not → haven't, 've not

　　has not → hasn't, 's not.

　　had not → hadn't

　　cannot → can't(can not 通常連在一起拼寫成 cannot)

　　could not → couldn't

　　may not → mayn't(美式英語幾乎完全不用此略寫(讀)式)

　　might not → mightn't

　　must not → mustn't

　　shall not → shan't(美式英語幾乎完全不用此略寫(讀)式)

　　should not → shouldn't

　　will not → won't

　　would not → wouldn't

11.1.3.　只含普通動詞的句子

肯定句　　　　否定句

主詞＋動詞…→主詞＋$\begin{Bmatrix} \text{do} \\ \text{does} \\ \text{did} \end{Bmatrix}$＋not＋動詞原形…

例如：

1. I *go* jogging every morning.　我每天早上慢跑。

　　　　I *do not go* jogging every morning.　我每天早上不慢跑。

　　2. She *likes* swimming.　她喜歡游泳。

　　　　She *does not like* swimming.　她不喜歡游泳。

　　3. They *lost* ten dollars.　他們失去了十元。

　　　　They *did not lose* ten dollars.　他們沒有失去十元。

do 與 not 也經常可略寫(讀)：

　　do＋not → don't

　　does＋not → doesn't

　　did＋not → didn't

11.2.　No、Not＋⒜NP、Never、None 等

　　以上 11.1. 節所描述的「**動詞組加 not**」方式，是**最普遍的否定法**。除此以外，英語還可以利用其他具有否定語意的語詞來構成否定句。這些否定語詞可大致分為兩種。本節討論 no、not＋⒜NP、none、及 never。下一節討論另一種否定詞語如 seldom、scarcely、hardly 等。

　　no、not ＋⒜NP、none、never、及 neither 本身具有否定的語意，可用於句子中，形成否定句。例如：

　　1. *No* one is here.　沒有人在這兒。

　　2. I see *no* dogs here.　我在這兒沒看到狗。

　　3. *No* honest man would lie.　誠實的人不說謊。

　　4. This is *no* good.　這不好。

　　5. They would said *not* a word.　他們一句話也不說。

　　6. He wasted *not* a minute.　他一分鐘也不浪費。

　　7. *Not* many people have come.　沒有很多人來。

8. *Not* one guest arrived on time. 沒有一個客人準時到。

9. *None* of us wanted to go home. 我們當中沒有人想回家。

10. *None* of the typewriters is ／ are mine. 沒有一部打字機是我的。

11. *Neither* of them wanted to leave. 他們兩人都不想離開。

12. I will *never* let him use my car again. 我再也不會讓他用我的車子。

注意: (1)從上面例句得知 no 可以直接修飾名詞, 但 not 則不可。not 常加 a 或其他數量詞如 many 等才可與名詞連用。

(2)除少數如 no good, no different 等定形的片語外, no 修飾形容詞時, 只修飾比較級。試比較:

a. This plan is *no* good. 這個計劃不好。

b. If our plan is not good, theirs will be *no better.* 如果我們的計劃不好, 那麼他們的也不會比我們的好。

11.3. Seldom、Rarely、Hardly 等

seldom '很少'、rarely '很少'、scarcely '幾乎不'、barely '幾乎不'、little '很少'、few '很少' 等語詞, 其形式並非否定, 但語意卻為否定。這些語詞也可使句子成為否定句。例如:

1. I *seldom* go fishing. 我很少去釣魚。

2. He *hardly* ate anything. 他幾乎沒吃東西。

3. We *barely* had time to catch the bus. 我們幾乎趕不上那班公車。(時間幾乎不夠)

4. I saw *scarcely* any one. 我幾乎看不到有人。

5. She *rarely* comes here.　她很少來這兒。

6. He has *little* interest in English.　他對英語沒什麼興趣。

7. *Few* of the guests were having fun.　沒幾個客人玩得開心。

8. He has very *few* books.　他沒有多少本書。(幾乎沒有)

11.4.　含 no、hardly 等否定語詞的句子的附加短問句

　　含有 no、hardly 等語詞的句子，雖然其動詞爲肯定式，但因爲實際的語意爲否定，所以如要加附加短問句時，要用肯定的附加短問句。例如：

1. I *hardly* have any time, *do I?*　我幾乎沒時間，對嗎？

2. His plan is *no* good, *is it?*　他的計劃不好，對嗎？

3. I see *no* dogs here, *do I?*　我在這兒看不到狗，對嗎？

4. She is *no* friend of yours, *is she?* 她不是你的朋友，對嗎？

《習題 15》

(A)將下列各句改成否定句。用兩種或三種方式：(1)用非略寫式；(2)用 n't 略寫式；(3)如有兩種略寫式的助動詞，用 n't 以外的另一種略寫式。

例： He is a student.

He *is not* a student.

He *isn't* a student.

He*'s not* a student.

1. Adam looks like his mother.

2. I am busy.

3. I like him.

4. We must go to school tomorrow.

5. Mary has lived here for ten years.

6. I would like to have some coffee.

7. They had to work hard.

8. We are planning to go abroad.

9. We must open the door at once.

10. Stay here.

11. He is washing his hands.

12. They will arrive on time.

13. They are angry with you.

14. We were nervous.

15. We lost a hundred dollars.

(B)填入 no 或 not。

1. _____ man would say such a thing to him.

2. I understand _____ a word of English.

3. I will _____ give you my umbrella.

4. There is _____ time for that.

5. She is _____ more beautiful than you.

6. I am _____ going to wait any longer.

7. _____ many people came to the meeting.

8. Chris is _____ a friend of mine.

9. He would say _____ a word.

10. _____ one listens to me.

第十二章
名詞

12.1.　簡介人稱、數、性、及格

英語的名詞及代名詞具有好幾種構詞及文法上的特性，就是**人稱**(person)、**數**(number)、**性**(gender)及**格**(case)。這些特性，是英語文法中重要的部分。

12.1.1.　人稱

人稱可分三種：
第一人稱(first person)：說話者
第二人稱(second person)：聽話者(對話者)
第三人稱(third person)：談及之人或事、物

12.1.2.　數

英語只區別兩種數：「**單數**」(singular　number)表示「一」。「**複數**」

(plural number)表示「多於一」。

12.1.3.　性

英語文法中的性(gender)可分爲：

(1)**陽性**(masculine gender)　指雄性的人或動物名詞。如 boy、man。

(2)**陰性**(feminine　gender)　指雌性的人或動物名詞。如 girl、woman。

(3)**中性**(neuter　gender)　指無性別可分及無生命的事物的名詞。如 desk、chair。

(4)**通性**(common　gender)　指雄性或雌性的人或動物的名詞。如 child、parent。

12.1.4.　格

英語文法有三種格(case)。句子的主詞、主詞補語、主詞同位語、直接稱謂的名詞爲「**主格**」(nominative case)。受詞、受詞補語、介詞受詞、受詞同位語的名詞爲「**受格**」(accusative case)。置於另一名詞前面，表示所有者或領屬者的名詞爲「**所有格**」(possessive case)。

12.2.　名詞的種類

名詞是人、地、事、物或概念的名稱，在文法功能上常作主詞或受詞，詞形上則有單複數及所有格的變化。

名詞可分爲：「專有名詞」、「普通名詞」、「抽象名詞」、「物質名詞」、「集

合名詞」等五種。

　(1)**專有名詞**(proper noun)是特定的人、地、事物、節慶等的名稱，拼寫時要以**大寫字母起首**。例如：Peter、Mary、Larry、Edward、Taipei '臺北'、Hong Kong '香港'、Singapore '新加坡'、New York '紐約'、London '倫敦'、Sunday '星期天'、October '十月'、Christmas '聖誕節' 等。

　(2)**普通名詞**(common noun)是一般(而非特定)的人、地、事、物共同的名稱。拼寫時不必以大寫開始。例如：boy '男孩子'、girl '女孩子'、man '男人'、dog '狗'、city '城市'、chair '椅子'、apple '蘋果'、map '地圖' 等。

　(3)**物質名詞**(mass noun, 或稱 material noun)指構成物體的不可分的質及材料等。例如：water '水'、air '空氣'、coffee '咖啡'、iron '鐵'、wool '羊毛'、paper '紙'、milk '牛奶'、bread '麵包' 等。

　(4)**抽象名詞**(abstract noun)為事物的性質、特性、以及抽象的想法、概念等的名稱。例如：love '愛'、beauty '美'、courage '勇氣'、happiness '幸福'、honesty '誠實' 等。

　(5)**集合名詞**(collective noun)為一群人、動物、或事物整體的名稱。例如：crowd '群眾'、team '隊'、class '班'、committee '委員會'、herd '獸群'、party '政黨'、family '家庭' 等。

12.3.　名詞的數

英語的名詞有單數與複數之分。複數通常表示「多於一」，單數通常表示「一」。在詞形上，單數名詞通常不加任何變化，複數(除不規則者以外)通常加複數字尾 {-s}。

　　一般說來，有複數形式的名詞大多數是普通名詞。如果我們以是否可以有複數形式來區分名詞，可以把名詞分為「可數名詞」(count noun, 可以有複數)以及「不可數名詞」(non-count noun, 不可以有複數)兩種。大體上抽象名詞、物質名詞多屬不可數名詞，而普通名詞通常為可數名詞。

12.3.1.　規則複數形式

⑴大多數名詞可在單數形式後加字尾-s，形成複數。例如：

單數	複數		單數	複數	
book	books	書	room	rooms	房間
apple	apples	蘋果	cap	caps	帽子
pen	pens	筆	cat	cats	貓
desk	desks	桌子	actor	actors	演員
pencil	pencils	鉛筆	game	games	遊戲
dog	dogs	狗	cab	cabs	計程車
bud	buds	花蕊	girl	girls	女孩子

⑵名詞字尾發音為 [s]、[z]、[ʃ]、[ʒ]、[tʃ]，及 [dʒ]，加字尾-es 而形成複數。[注意：這些發音通常由字母 s、z、x、sh、ch、ge 等拼寫] 例

如:

單數	複數		單數	複數	
rose	roses	玫瑰	box	boxes	箱子
bus	buses	公車	bridge	bridges	橋
buzz	buzzes	嗡嗡聲	ditch	ditches	溝
church	churches	教室	brush	brushes	刷子
village	villages	鄉村	garage	garages	車庫

注意: 字尾拼寫成 ch 但唸 [k] 的字, 加-s。例如: stomach(胃), stomachs。

⑶字尾爲字母 y 者。

A. 子音＋y 時, y 改爲 i 再加-es。例如:

單數	複數		單數	複數	
baby	babies	嬰兒	copy	copies	副本
century	centuries	世紀	country	countries	國家
family	families	家庭❶	sky	skies	天空
quality	qualities	品質	fly	flies	蒼蠅

B. 字尾爲母音＋y 者, 只加-s。例如:

單數	複數		單數	複數	
key	keys	鑰匙	day	days	天

---

❶ family (committee 等)當作普通名詞時, 要加複數字尾才能當複數用, 解釋作「不只一個家庭」。但當集合名詞使用時, 其單數形式可指集合中的個體, 而與複數動詞連用。例如, My family are all well. ‘我全家人都安好’。

monkey　monkeys　猴子　　　boy　　　boys　　　男孩

注意：字尾爲 y 的專有名詞如要表示複數時，也是只加-s。例如：two
Marys '兩個瑪莉'、two Germanys '兩個德國'。

⑷字尾爲 o 者，有三種方式。

A. 加-s。例如：

單數	複數		單數	複數	
radio	radios	收音機	studio	studios	攝影室
zoo	zoos	動物園	piano	pianos	鋼琴
photo	photos	照片	kilo	kilos	公斤
Filipino	Filipinos	菲律賓人	Eskimo	Eskimos	愛斯基摩人

B. 加-es。例如：

單數	複數		單數	複數	
hero	heroes	英雄	potato	potatoes	馬鈴薯
echo	echoes	回聲	tomato	tomatoes	蕃茄
topedo	topedoes	魚雷	negro	negroes	黑人

C. 加-s 或-es 均可。例如：

單數	複數		單數	複數	
buffalo	buffalos buffaloes	水牛	cargo	cargos cargoes	貨物
mosquito	mosquitos mosquitoes	蚊子	volcano	volcanos volcanoes	火山

注意：這三種情形的名詞，並不容易歸納出實用而好記的法則，如有疑

慮時，最好的方法就是查字典。

(5)字尾拼成 f 或 fe(發音爲 [f])，把 f 改爲 v，加-es。例如：

單數	複數		單數	複數	
wife	wives	妻子	knife	knives	刀子
life	lives	生命	thief	thieves	小偷
shelf	shelves	架子	wolf	wolves	狼
leaf	leaves	葉子	half	halves	半
loaf	loaves	條、塊 (麵包)			

注意：有兩種例外，

　　　(a)只加-s 者。如：

belief	beliefs	信仰	chief	chiefs	主管
safe	safes	保險箱	roof	roofs	屋頂

　　　(b)加-s 或變爲-ves 均可者。例如：

dwarf	dwarfs	dwarves	侏儒
scarf	scarfs	scarves	圍巾
wharf	wharfs	wharves	碼頭

(6)字母、略語或數目字之複數加's。例如：

one q	一個 q 字母	two q's	兩個 q 字母
one Ph.D.	一個博士學位	three Ph.D.'s	三個博士學位
1980's	八十年代		

12.3.2. 規則複數字尾-s 或-es 的發音

⑴單數名詞字尾發[s]、[z]、[ʃ]、[ʒ]、[tʃ]、[dʒ]等嘶音時，-s 或-es 字尾發 [ɪz]。例如：

bus [-s]	buses [-ɪz]	公車
buzz [-z]	buzzes [-ɪz]	嗡嗡聲
toothbrush [-ʃ]	toothbrushes [-ɪz]	牙刷
garage [-ʒ]	garages [-ɪz]	車庫
church [-tʃ]	churches [-ɪz]	教堂
bridge [-dʒ]	bridges [-ɪz]	橋

⑵單數名詞字尾發無聲子音(或稱「清子音」voiceless consonant)，而又不是⑴所述之嘶音時，複數字尾-s 發音為 [-s]。例如：

hope [-p]	hopes [-s]	希望
coat [-t]	coats [-s]	外衣
desk [-k]	desks [-s]	桌子
cliff [-f]	cliffs [-s]	山崖
month [-θ]	months [-s]	月

⑶單數名詞字尾發音為母音或有聲子音(或稱為「濁子音」voiced consonant)，而又不是上面⑴所述之嘶音時，複數字尾-s 發 [-z]。例如：

cab [-b]	cabs [-z]	計程車
bud [-d]	buds [-z]	花蕊
dog [-g]	dogs [-z]	狗
cave [-v]	caves [-z]	洞穴

doll 〔-l〕	dolls 〔-z〕	洋娃娃
dollar 〔-r〕	dollars 〔-z〕	元
game 〔-m〕	games 〔-z〕	遊戲
pen 〔-n〕	pens 〔-z〕	筆
king 〔-ŋ〕	kings 〔-z〕	國王
sea 〔-i〕	seas 〔-z〕	海
family 〔-ɪ〕	families 〔-z〕	家庭
day 〔-e〕	days 〔-z〕	天
potato 〔-o〕	potatoes 〔-z〕	馬鈴薯
shoe 〔-u〕	shoes 〔-z〕	鞋子

12.3.3. 不規則複數

⑴以母音變化形成複數。例如:

單數	複數		單數	複數	
man	men	男人	woman	women	女人
foot	feet	腳	tooth	teeth	牙齒
goose	geese	鵝	louse	lice	蝨子
mouse	mice	老鼠			

⑵有些名詞加-en 形成複數。例如:

單數	複數		單數	複數	
ox	oxen	公牛	child	children	小孩

⑶有些名詞單數複數形式相同。
A. 有些動物的名詞, 如 fish '魚'、deer '鹿'、cod '鱈魚' 等。

B. 國籍名詞中，字尾為-ese 者，如：

Chinese 中國人	one Chinese	two Chinese
Japanese 日本人	one Japanese	two Japanese
Portuguese 葡萄牙人	one Portuguese	two Portuguese
Lebanese 黎巴嫩人	one Lebanese	two Lebanese
Vietnamese 越南人	one Vietnamese	two Vietnamese

另外，Swiss '瑞士人' 也是單複數同形，不加字尾。

C. 數量詞如 dozen '打'、hundred '百'、thousand '千' 等如前面另有數詞修飾時，其複數不加-s。例如：

two *dozen* eggs　二打蛋

three *thousand* people　三千人

four *hundred* times　四百倍、四百次

five *million* dollars　五百萬元

We want six *hundred*.　我們要六百。

They only want two *million*(*s*). 他們只想要兩百萬。(million 後面如果沒有其他名詞時，可以加-s)

另外，名詞前面加數詞而作修飾語時，該名詞也不加-s。例如：

a *ten-story* building　一幢十層的樓房

a *two-month* holiday　一個為期兩個月的假期

a *five-hour* speech　一場五個鐘頭的演說

(4)外來名詞

英語中有些從拉丁文、希臘文、法文、意大利文借用的名詞。這些名詞有些成為英文中的常用語詞，這些字的複數形成常有兩種，一種是不規則的複數(即保留其外來字的原來複數形式)，另一種是規則的複數(即以英語規則字尾-s 或-es 形成)。外來複數形式常用於正式與技術性質的文字中，而規

則的複數形式則用於平常的使用場合。然而，一般說來，這些外來語詞對初學者而言，大多數都算比較艱深少用。我們只舉以下幾則爲例：

單數	複數	
focus	*foci, focuses*	焦點
curriculum	*curricula、curriculums*	課程
basis	*bases*	基礎
analysis	*analyses*	分析
formula	*formulae、formulas*	公式

12.3.4.　名詞的「數」應注意的事項

⑴有些字的字尾爲-s，但通常只作單數用，這些字通常爲：

學科名稱：mathematics　'數學'、physics　'物理'、economics '經濟學' 等。

疾病名稱：measles　'痲疹'、mumps　'腮腺炎' 等。

遊戲運動名稱：billiards　'撞球'、darts　'擲鏢' 等。

另外，news '消息' 也屬這類名詞。

　　1. *Mathematics* is his favorite subject.
　　　數學是他喜愛的學科。

　　2. *Darts* is popular among young people.
　　　擲鏢是年輕人流行的遊戲。

⑵表示**由兩部分合成的工具、器具及衣物的名詞，通常爲複數**。例如：

glasses	眼鏡	scissors	剪刀
braces	吊帶(英式英語)	suspenders	吊帶(美式)
jeans	牛仔褲	pants	褲子

| shorts | 短褲 | pajamas | 睡衣 |
| trousers | 褲子　等 | | |

⑶有些名詞並沒有複數標記，但通常只當作複數使用。例如：people '人，人們'、folk '人，人們'、police '警方'、cattle '牲口' 等。

　　1. Many *people* have come.　很多人已經來了。

　　注意：people 當作 '民族、國家' 解釋時，為單數，其複數也可加-s。
　　　　　例如：

　　　　　They are *a* great *people*.　他們是一個偉大的民族。

　　　　　the English speaking *peoples*　說英語的民族

　　2. The *police* have caught the thief.　警方已經逮捕到小偷了。

12.3.5.　不可數名詞

　　不可數名詞主要有兩種：⑴「抽象名詞」：如 knowledge '知識'、honesty '誠實'、kindness '好意'、courage '勇氣'、freedom '自由'、childhood '兒童時代'、love '愛'、time '時間'、width '寬度'、length '長度' 等。⑵「物質名詞」：如 gold '金'、iron '鐵'、silver '銀'、water '水'、wood '木'、stone '石'、sand '沙'、air '空氣'、wool '羊毛'、metal '金屬'、meat '肉'、bread '麵包' 等。

　　「抽象名詞」通常不具體而且也不易個別化。而「物質名詞」雖然具體，但也不易個別化或個體化。因此，這兩種名詞在英語中都屬不可數名詞。

　　不可數名詞在文法上的特點是：在正常的用法中，沒有複數形式。

⑴抽象名詞

　　A. 抽象名詞常表示概念、狀態、品質、活動等。例如：

kindness	好意	happiness	幸福
music	音樂	history	歷史
friendship	友誼	arrival	到達　等

B. 抽象名詞沒有複數。例如:

1. She showed him much *kindness*.　她對他表示很大的善意。
2. The *arrival* of the train has been delayed.
　　火車的抵達已經延遲了。

但是，如果是表示具有抽象名詞的性質的個別例子或現象時(無論是人或物)，也可以當作可數名詞。例如:

3. She showed him many *kindnesses*.　她對他表示很多善意的行為。
4. She was *a* late *arrival*.　她是一位遲來者。

C. 一些常見的抽象名詞字尾:

-ness、-ity、-ty、-th、-dom、-hood、-ship、-ism、-al、-ation、-ment、-ion 等，是常用的字尾，常加在形容詞、名詞或動詞後面，形成抽象名詞。例如:

kindness	好意	safety	安全
ability	能力	growth	生長
wisdom	智慧	boyhood	少年時代
friendship	友誼	arrival	到達
freedom	自由	movement	動態
examination	考試、檢查	等	

(2)物質名詞

A.物質名詞不加-s，不與 a 或 an 連用。泛稱時也不加冠詞。例如：

1. *Iron* is useful.　鐵是有用的。

2. He bought some *bread*.　他買了些麵包。

3. I don't have any *money*.　我沒有錢。

4. We all need *water* and *air*.　我們都需要水與空氣。

B.**物質名詞不能直接與數詞**(numerals)**連用。表示數量時，數詞與物質名詞之間要有量詞**(classifiers)，如 cup '杯'、bit '一點'、piece '張、塊'、bar '塊'、loaf '條'、pound '磅' 等。例如：

a bar of soap　一塊肥皂

two bars of chocolate　兩塊巧克力

a bit of wood　一小塊木頭

two pieces of chalk　兩枝粉筆

a piece of news　一則消息

a loaf of bread　一塊(條)麵包

a bag of rice　一袋米

two bottles of wine　兩瓶酒

three pounds of meat　三磅肉

這情形也適用於抽象名詞。例如：

a bit of luck　一點運氣

a ray of hope　一線希望

C. 物質名詞前面可用 much、little、及 some，但不能用 many 或 a few。例如：

much money　　＊ many money

some water　　＊ a few water

little gold　　＊ many gold

(3)專有名詞

專有名詞通常不用複數形式。但如遇有同名的人或地時，則可加複數字尾-s。一般說來專有名詞除字尾為 x、s、z、ch、sh 加-es 外，其餘都加-s。字母 y 結尾的專有名詞也是加-s。例如：

We have one John, two Marys and three Alices in our class.
　我們班上有一個John，兩個Mary，三個Alice。

另外，有關專有名詞，我們還有以下幾點應注意的事項：

A. the＋專有名詞可表示「名叫…的一家人」。例如：

　the Smiths　Smith 一家人

　the Wangs　王家(一家人)

　the Joneses　Jones 一家人

B. 專有名詞要以大寫字母起首，如頭銜緊接於名字之前，頭銜也應大寫起首。例如：

*G*eorge *B*ush　喬治布希

*M*r. *B*ush　布希先生

*P*resident *B*ush　布希總統

12.4.　名詞的人稱

英語名詞的人稱並無詞形上的分別。一般說來，除了在直接稱謂所用的

名詞, 或與第一人稱代名詞(I、we)同位的同位語以外, 其他名詞都是**第三人稱**。例如:

    1. *Students* should do their homework.　學生應該做功課。

    2. *This book* is expensive.　這本書很貴。

用於直接稱謂之名詞可作**第二人稱**, 例如:

    3. I'd like to have a word with you, *Mr. Wang*.　王先生，我想跟你談一談。

第一人稱代名詞之同位語可作**第一人稱**, 例如:

    4. *We young people* like pop music.　我們年輕人喜歡流行音樂。

12.5.　名詞的性

    英語名詞的性(gender)分爲陽性、陰性、通性、及中性四種。其中前三種是指「有生命」(animate)的名詞, 中性是指「無生命」(inanimate)的名詞。在英語的文法中, 名詞的性比較重要的功能是決定代名詞的形式, 如 man～he／him／ his(陽性), woman～she／her／her(陰性)等。

12.5.1.　陰性與陽性名詞的形式

    中性與通性名詞字形上並無區別, 其代名詞用 it／they 等。陰性與陽性名詞很多是指屬人(human)的「有生名詞」(animate noun), 也有些是指動物的有生名詞。

    (1)陰性陽性字形相同的名詞。

陽性	陰性	
artist	*artist*	藝術家
assistant	*assistant*	助理
cook	*cook*	廚子
dancer	*dancer*	舞者
driver	*driver*	駕駛員
doctor	*doctor*	醫生

(2)陰性陽性字形不相同的名詞。

A.加字尾 -ess、-ine 而形成陰性。

陽性		陰性	
actor	男演員	*actress*	女演員
conductor	男車掌	*conductress*	女車掌
duke	公爵	*duchess*	公爵夫人
heir	男繼承人	*heiress*	女繼承人
emperor	皇帝	*empress*	女皇
god	神	*goddess*	女神
host	男主人	*hostess*	女主人
waiter	男侍者	*waitress*	女侍者
prince	王子	*princess*	公主
lion	公獅	*lioness*	母獅
tiger	公老虎	*tigress*	母老虎
hero	英雄	*heroine*	女英雄

B. 不加字尾變化者。

1.第一類:

陽性		陰性	
man	男人	*woman*	女人
boy	男孩	*girl*	女孩
brother	兄弟	*sister*	姊妹
father	父	*mother*	母
gentleman	紳士	*lady*	淑女，女士
husband	丈夫	*wife*	妻子
male	男性	*female*	女性
nephew	姪子	*niece*	姪女
son	兒子	*daughter*	女兒
king	國王	*queen*	皇后
uncle	叔、伯、舅	*aunt*	嬸母、伯母、舅母
bull	公牛	*cow*	母牛
cock,rooster	公雞	*hen*	母雞
dog	公狗	*bitch*	母狗
drake	公鴨	*duck*	母鴨
gander	公鵝	*goose*	母鵝
stallion	公馬	*mare*	母馬

2.第二類: 含有第一類的複合名詞。

陽性		陰性	
boyfriend	男朋友	*girlfriend*	女朋友
grandfather	祖父	*grandmother*	祖母
grandson	孫子	*granddaughter*	孫女
father-in-law	岳父／公公	*mother-in-law*	岳母／婆婆

salesman	男店員/男推銷員	*saleswoman*	女店員/女推銷員
man-servant	男僕人	*maid-serv-ant*	女僕人
landlord	男房東	*landlady*	女房東
he-goat	公山羊	*she-goat*	母山羊
male-frog	雄青蛙	*female-frog*	雌青蛙　等

12.5.2.　名詞的性與代名詞

⑴對屬人單數名詞而言, 指男性者用 he／him／his, 指女性者用 she／her。通性名詞如確知所提是男或女時用 he 或 she, 否則通常用 he。例如:

1. The ***boy*** is talking to ***his*** mother.　那個男孩子正在跟他母親說話。

2. Do you see the ***girl*** over there?　***She*** is my eldest sister. 你看見在那邊的那個女孩子嗎? 她是我大姐。

3. The ***artist*** took off ***his***／***her*** overcoat.　那位藝術家把他／她的外衣脫下。

4. A ***driver*** should take good care of ***his*** car.　駕駛員應該好好照顧他的車子。(泛稱所有駕駛員)

注意: baby 與 child(特別是 baby)因性別不易判別, 常用 it／its 為代名詞。例如: The ***baby*** and ***its*** mother are here。但是, 對嬰兒的父母親來說, 因為早知其性別, 所以很少會用 it／its。例如: "***My baby*** is cute, isn't ***she***／***he***?" the mother said.　那位母親說:「我的小寶貝很可愛, 不是嗎?」

⑵無生命單數的代名詞為 it／its。

I bought a ***book*** yesterday but I lost ***it*** this morning.　我昨

天買了一本書但是今天早上把它弄丟了。

(3)指動物的代名詞常用 it／its。例如：

1. I don't like that *dog* because *it* likes to bark all the time. 我不喜歡那隻狗，因爲它喜歡不停地吠。

但比較柔順的動物則常可用 she／her 爲代名詞。例如：

2. Tom has a *cat* and he likes *her* very much.　Tom 有一隻貓，他很喜歡她。

(4)船(或其他交通工具名詞)、國家等名詞常用陰性代名詞。例如：

1. *China* lost many of *her* bravest soldiers during the Sino-Japanese War.　中國在中日戰爭中失去很多她的最英勇的軍人。

2. Look at the *ship*. Isn't *she* beautiful?　你看看那條船。她不是很美麗嗎？

(5)在文學作品或童話故事中，因「擬人化」的用法，常把較剛陽、強壯之事物當男性，而把柔順、細小、優美之事物當女性。例如：

A.**陽性**

sun '太陽'、*mountain* '山'、*summer* '夏天'、*winter* '冬天'、*war* '戰爭'、*anger* '憤怒'、*day* '白天' 等(代名詞用 he ／him／his)。

B.**陰性**

moon '月亮'、*nature* '大自然'、*earth* '地球'、*ship* '船'、*spring* '春天'、*autumn* '秋天'、*night* '夜'、*country* '國家'、*art* '藝術'、*music* '音樂'、*pity* '同情' 等(代名詞用 she／her／her)。

12.6.　名詞的格

　　從字形上看, 英語只有「所有格」有明顯的字尾 's 表示。「主格」與「受格」在字形上完全相同, 也不加任何字尾或字頭, 因此, 對於主格與受格名詞, 我們只說明其在句子中的文法功能。

12.6.1.　主格與受格

⑴具有以下文法功能的名詞或名詞組爲主格:

A.主詞

　　John is a student.　John 是學生。

B.主詞補語

　　John is a *scientist*.　John 是科學家。

C.直接稱謂(vocatives)

　　1. *Boys,* be quiet.　孩子們, 不要吵。

　　2. Come here, *John*.　John, 來這裏。

D.主詞的同位語

　　Larry, *my son*, is an excellent cook.

　　我的兒子 Larry 是一位非常好的廚師。

⑵具有下列文法功能的名詞爲受格:

A.動詞的受詞

　　1. I gave the man *a book*.　我給那個男人一本書。

　　2. I gave *the man* a book.

B.介詞的受詞

The book is on the *desk*.　這本書在桌子上。

C.受詞的同位語

I just saw Miss Lin, our new *secretary*.

我剛才看見我們的新秘書林小姐。

D.受詞補語

1. We elected him our *president*.　我們選他當我們的總統。
2. We consider him a good *teacher*.　我們認為他是一位好老師。

12.6.2.　所有格

一般說來，「有生名詞」多用「’s」或「’」表示所有格；「無生名詞」多用「of＋NP」表示所有格。

⑴有生名詞所有格有下列方式：

A.單數名詞後加「’s」(包括字尾為 s 的字)。

　the *cat’s* tail　貓的尾巴

　a *dog’s* eyes　狗的眼睛

　Mr. *Hope’s* pen　Hope 先生的筆

　Tom’s pet　Tom 的小寵物

　our *boss’s* son　我們老闆的兒子

　James’s friend　James 的朋友

B.複數名詞，字尾為 s 者加「’」，字尾不是 s 者則加「’s」。

　cats’ tails　貓的尾巴

　those *boys’* overcoats　那些男孩們的外套

birds' wings　鳥兒的翅膀

children's education　兒童的教育

the *Taylors'* residences　（幾位）Taylors的寓所（單數為Taylor）

C.共同所有與個別所有：

⒜共同所有在最後名詞加「's」：

Peter and Larry's house　Peter 與 Larry 共有的房子

⒝個別所有則在每個所有者的名詞加「's」：

Peter's and *Larry's* books　Peter 的書以及 Larry 的書（各自不同的書）

⑵無生名詞的所有格。

無生名詞的所有格通常以「of＋名詞」表示。例如：

　　the name of the ship　這船的名字

　　the front of the house　屋子的前方

　　the cover of the book　書的封面

⑶有些無生名詞也可以用「's」表示所有格。

A.地理名詞

　洲：*Europe's* history　歐洲的歷史

　國家：*Canada's* population　加拿大的人口

　州：*California's* industry　加州的工業

　城市：*Taipei's* traffic　台北的交通

　大學：*Harvard's* Department of Psychology　哈佛大學的心理學系

B.處所、機關等名詞

　　the *hotel's* front door　飯店的前門

the ***world's*** history   世界的歷史

the ***earth's*** surface   地球的表面

the ***government's*** organization   政府的組織

C.時間、距離、重量、價值等名詞

today's newspaper   今天的報紙

a day's work   一天的工作

two weeks' vacation   兩週的假期

a mile's walk   一哩的步行

three pounds' weight   三磅的重量

ten dollars' worth   十元的價值

(4)獨立使用的所有格

含所有格的名詞組如語意清楚時，所有格後面的名詞可以省略。例如：

1. My car is more expensive than ***Mr. Wang's***. 我的車子比
   王先生的(車子)要貴。(Mr. Wang's ＝Mr. Wang's car)

2. This pen is ***Peter's***. 這枝筆是Peter的。(Peter's ＝ Peter's pen)

3. ***Nancy's*** was the prettiest dress. Nancy 的衣服是最漂亮的。
   (Nancy's ＝ Nancy's dress)

《習題 16》

(A)在下列句子中，把名詞指出，並標明其在句中的功能。使用以下的略寫方式。

S＝主詞   DO＝直接受詞   IO＝間接受詞

SComp＝主詞補語   OP＝介詞受詞

OComp＝受詞補語

例： _Tom_ gave _Mary_ a _book_ .
    S   IO   DO

1. The students in that class work hard.

2. The man paid the old woman five dollars for the magazine.

3. My son won a prize in the contest（比賽）.

4. Mr. Wang is a scientist.

5. The students consider Mary the best teacher in their school.

6. Tony sent his children to the shop.

(B)填入適當的複數。

   例： boy _boys_

1. baby _____   2. fox _____

3. key _____   4. deer _____

5. church _____   6. radio _____

7. potato _____   8. bush _____

9. piano _____   10. quality _____

11. leaf _____   12. shelf _____

13. roof _____   14. wife _____

15. hero _____   16. bus _____

17. goose _____   18. foot _____

(C)在下列各句中，將括號中的名詞複數寫出。

   例： There are two (boy).

      There are two _boys._   _boys_

1. They have five (child).   _____

2. We think that the (tax) are too high.   _____

3. I need three (tomato).   _____

4. We stayed in Hong Kong for two (month). ＿＿＿＿

5. We have visited several big (church) in England. ＿＿＿＿

6. The old man has no (tooth). ＿＿＿＿

7. I bought four (loaf) of bread. ＿＿＿＿

8. We have two (lawyer) in town. ＿＿＿＿

(D)以下各句中，將 of 片語改成「's」或「'」形式的所有格。

　例：John is the father of Clara.

　　→ John is Clara's father.

1. The parents of the children are here.

2. The apartment of Mr. Jones has been sold.

3. The crew(水手) of the ship decided to jump overboard.

4. She likes the attitudes (態度) of her friends.

5. The rays of the sun shine on the island.

6. The boy tried to pull the tail of the dog.

7. The hair of the man is too long.

8. The reputation (名譽) of my cousin is not very good.

(E)填入一適當的數量詞。

　例：He drank a *cup* of water. (或 glass)

　　He drank two *cups* of water. (或 glasses)

1. Please give me a ＿＿＿＿ of soap.

2. She bought two ＿＿＿＿ of bread.

3. I want three ＿＿＿＿ of meat.

4. We need a ＿＿＿＿ of chalk.

5. They bought several ＿＿＿＿ of furniture.

6. He got a ＿＿＿＿ of chocolate.

7. Tom wants a _____ of milk.

(F)填入陽性或陰性名詞。

陽性	陰性
1. actor	_____
2. heir	_____
3._____	lioness
4. waiter	_____
5. emperor	_____
6._____	goddess
7. tiger	_____
8. hero	_____
9. boy	_____
10. dog	_____
11. king	_____
12._____	mother
13._____	mare
14. boyfriend	_____
15. he-goat	_____
16._____	granddaughter

第十三章
代名詞

13.1. 代名詞的種類

　　簡單地說, 代名詞(Pronoun)就是「代替名詞的語詞」。很多時候, 我們為了避免名詞的重複使用, 會用代名詞來代替名詞。例如:

John is a student and John goes to school every day.

我們會寫成　John is a student and he goes to school every day.

　　一般說來, 代名詞可分以下幾種:

1. **人稱代名詞**(Personal Pronouns)
2. **反身代名詞**(Reflexive Pronouns)
3. **指示代名詞**(Demonstrative Pronouns)
4. **不定代名詞**(Indefinite Pronouns)
5. **相互代名詞**(Reciprocal Pronouns)
6. **疑問代名詞**(Interrogative Pronouns)
7. **關係代名詞**(Relative Pronouns)

　　在這幾種代名詞中, 疑問代名詞在〈問句的形成〉一章中已有敍述, 關係代名詞在另一章(〈關係子句〉)中再加討論。本章以其餘五種代名詞為重

點。疑問代名詞及關係代名詞只是簡略提出，並不詳細討論。

13.2. 人稱代名詞

人稱代名詞的形式

		第一人稱		第二人稱		第三人稱			
		單數	複數	單數	複數	單數陽性	單數陰性	單數中性	複數
主	格	I	we	you	you	he	she	it	they
受	格	me	us	you	you	him	her	it	them
所有格	限定用法	my	our	your	your	his	her	its	their
	獨立用法	mine	ours	yours	yours	his	hers	its	theirs

人稱代名詞用法應注意以下各項。

13.2.1. 格的用法

(1)主格代名詞用作主詞及主詞補語。受格代名詞用作受詞、介詞受詞。例如：

1. *I* was at home yesterday. （主詞）我昨天在家。
2. Mr. Wang saw *her*. （受詞）黃先生看見她。
3. You are sitting on *it*. （介詞受詞）你正坐在它上面。

4. Who is there?　誰呀?

　　It's *I*. (主詞補語)是我。

　　(非正式用法與口語常說　It's *me*.)

⑵在涉及主詞比較的比較句中, than 與 as 後面的代名詞正式的用法是用主格, 但口語及非正式用法中也容許受格。例如:

1. He is more diligent than *she*.　他比她更勤勉。(... than she is diligent)

2. He is as tall as *she*.　他跟她一樣高。(... as she is tall)

3. He is more diligent than *her*. 他比她更勤勉。(口語／非正式)

4. He is as tall as *her*. 他跟她一樣高。(口語／非正式)

注意: 在口語中1、2 兩句聽起來太正式而不自然。但如在 she 後面加上 be 動詞(或在其他情形下加上助動詞), 聽起來就比較自然些。例如 He is more diligent than she is. He can swim faster than she can. 等。

⑶所有格代名詞有兩種用法。

⒜**限定用法**(determinative), 其功能像一般的形容詞及定詞, 主要置於名詞前面。例如:

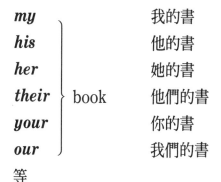

my		我的書
his		他的書
her		她的書
their	book	他們的書
your		你的書
our		我們的書
等		

　　(b)**獨立用法**(independent)，其用法與獨立名詞所有格的用法相似。例如：

　　1. This is **_John's_** book. (限定用法，名詞所有格)　這是 John 的書。

　　2. This book is **_John's._** (獨立用法，名詞所有格)　這本書是 John 的。

　　3. This is **_my_** book. (限定用法，代名詞所有格)　這是我的書。

　　4. This book is **_mine._** (獨立用法，代名詞所有格)　這本書是我的。

　　⑷ own 可以加強代名詞所有格的語氣。但 own 只能用於 my、his、her、our、your、their、its(亦即限定用法所有格)後面。例如：

　　1. I want **_my own_** copy.　我要我自己的副本。

　　2. He cooks **_his own_** dinner.　他自己煮自己的晚飯。

13.2.2.　代名詞的人稱

代名詞的人稱相當明確，每種人稱都有特別的字形表示。

　　第一人稱(說話者)：I、we (受格 me、us)

　　第二人稱(聽者)：you、you (受格 you、you)

　　第三人稱(被談及者)：he ／ she ／ it／they(受格 him ／ her ／ it／them)

代名詞為單數時，人稱很清楚明確。

代名詞為複數時，其指稱如含(Ｉ)則用第一人稱，如含聽者(you)則用第二人稱。如只含被談及者時，用第三人稱。例如：

　　1. **_John_** and **_I_** were absent yesterday. We were ill. John 和我

昨天缺席。我們生病了。

2. *You* and *Ann* should take care of *yourselves.* 你和 Ann 應該照顧你們自己。

3. *Tom* and *Peter* are good friends. *They* are also class-mates. Tom 和 Peter 是好朋友，他們也是同班同學。

13.2.3. 人稱代名詞的性與數

人稱代名詞的性(gender)與數(number)取決於其指稱(先行詞，亦即其所指之名詞)。例如：John——he、him 等；Mary——she, her 等；the students——they、them 等。

一般說來，代名詞的性及數不難決定。唯一困難的是指稱爲不定代名詞(如 everyone '每個人'、everybody '每個人'、someone '某人'、some-body '某人'、anyone '任何人'、anybody '任何人'、no one '沒有人'、nobody '沒有人' 等。)英語在傳統文法上正式用法中用 *he* 來指稱這些不定代名詞。例如：

1. *Everyone* should bring *his* book to class. 每個人都應該把自己的書帶到班上來。

但近年來非正式用法也接受複數代名詞。例如：

2. *Everybody* came to my house, and *they* all came hap-pily. 每個人都到我家裡來，而且他們都是高高興興地來。

3. *Everyone* thinks that *they* have a right to come here. 每人都認爲他們有權到這兒來。

13.2.4. 人稱代名詞的一些特別用法

(1)三種人稱的複數代名詞都可以泛指「一般的人」。例如:

1. *We* should love *our* parents. 我們(人)都應該愛父母。

2. *You* can never be sure what will happen tomorrow.
   你們(人)永遠不能確知明天會有什麼事情發生。

3. *They* say it is going to rain tonight. 他們(人們／大家)說今晚上會下雨。

(2) It 可指天氣、時間、距離、或泛指一種情況, 或一個人、一件事等。例如:

1. *It*'s hot today. 今天很熱。

2. What time is *it*? 現在幾點了?
   It's one o'clock. 一點了。

3. How far is *it* from here to Taipei? 從這兒到臺北有多遠?
   It's about 20 kilometers. 大約 20 公里。

4. *It* is dark here. 這裡很黑。

5. Who is *it* ? (回應敲門)誰啊?
   It's me. 是我啊。
   或 *It*'s Tom and Alice. 是 Tom 和 Alice 啊。

(3) It 可在句子中作前導主詞或受詞(introductory subject／object)。這種主詞或受詞本身並無特別語意, 只是代表其後面的真正主詞或受詞(通常是不定詞或 that 子句)。例如:

1. *It* is important to study hard. 用功唸書是很重要的。(it=

to study hard)

2. *It* is fun to read novels.　看小說是有趣的事。(it＝to read novels)

3. I find *it* difficult to talk to him.　我發現要跟他談談並不容易。(it＝to talk to him)

13.3. 反身代名詞

反身代名詞(Reflexive Pronouns)有下列形式:

人稱＼數	單數	複數
第一人稱	myself	ourselves
第二人稱	yourself	yourselves
第三人稱	himself herself itself	themselves

反身代名詞主要用法有二:

⑴**作動詞的受詞以及介詞的受詞。**例如:

1. He hurt *himself.*　他傷害了自己。

2. She is looking at *herself* in the mirror.　她在照鏡子。(在鏡中看自己)

這是反身代名詞的最基本用法。亦即在同一句子中，主詞與受詞指同一人時，受詞要用反身代名詞。上面例句1之 himself 指與 he 為同一人，例2之 herself 與 she 是同一人。其他的例子如：

3. He enjoyed *himself*.　　他玩得很開心。

4. Larry killed *himself*.　　Larry 自殺了。

⑵強調用法

反身代名詞作主詞同位語時，可加強句子語氣，特別是加強主詞「本身」、「個人」的語氣。

1. I'll do it *myself*.　　我自己會做這事。

I *myself* will do it.

2. He *himself* made this choice.　　他自己作此選擇。

He made this choice *himself*.

13.4.　不定代名詞

13.4.1.

不代表或不指稱特別的人或事物的代名詞稱為「不定代名詞」(Indefinite Pronouns)。不定代名詞包括：

all	所有的人／物	*some*	有些人／物
any	任何人／物	*none*	無人／物
both	兩者(人／物)	*one*	一個(人／物)
either	兩者之一(人／物)	*neither*	兩者皆不(人／物)

each	各個(人／物)	*other*	其他的人／物
another	另一人／物	*few*	少數的人／物
little	少許，少量(事／物)	*many*	許多的人／物
much	很多，大量(事／物)		

以及「**複合不定代名詞**」(Compound Indefinite Pronouns)：

everyone	每人	*everybody*	每人
everything	一切，凡事	*someone*	某人
somebody	某人	*something*	某事
anyone	任何人	*anybody*	任何人
anything	任何事	*no one*	沒人
nobody	沒人	*nothing*	無事／物

以及 half '一半'、several '幾個(人／物)'、enough '足夠的人／物' 等。

這些不定代名詞通常在某一範圍內並不代表或指出特別某一個人或事物。例如：

1. ***Anyone*** in my class can answer that question.　我班上任何人都能回答這問題。

當然，不定代名詞也可泛指世上任何人或事物。例如：

2. ***No one*** can live without water.　沒有人可以沒有水而活下去。(沒有水人就活不下去，所有人都如此)

13.4.2.　不定代名詞用法上的一般注意事項

⑴提及不定代名詞時，通常使用第三人稱代名詞，其數與性視句意而定。如爲單數而性別不知時，正式用法用 he／his 等。例如：

1. ***Everyone*** has ***his*** own notebook.　每人都有自己的筆記本。

2. ***Each*** of the girls has ***her*** own notebook.　班上每個女孩子都有自己的筆記本。(從句中上下文已知是女性)

3. If you see ***anyone*** there, tell ***him*** to leave at once.　如果你在那兒看到任何人，叫他馬上離開。

4. ***Each*** of the books has ***its*** own value.　這些書中每一本都有它的價值。

5. I told ***both*** of the students to bring ***their*** own notebook.　我叫這兩個學生都把他們自己的筆記本帶來。

注意：上面13.2.3. 節已提到，在非正式用法及口語中，everyone、anyone 等不定代名詞也可用第三人稱複數代名詞代替。例如：

6. ***Everyone*** thinks that ***they*** have a right to come here.　每個人都認為他們有權來這兒。

(2)在語意上可以是單數也可以是複數的不定代名詞(如 all、most、some 等)，其數常視其後的 of 片語而定。例如：

1. All of the ***boys are*** here.　所有的男孩子都來了。

2. All of the ***meat was*** eaten.　所有的肉都被吃了。

3. Some of the ***soldiers were*** wounded.　有些士兵受了傷。

4. Some of the ***milk is*** sour.　這些牛奶中有一些是酸的。

不定代名詞本身語意也是決定其「數」的主要因素。例如, all 表示「所有的人」時用複數：

All are present.　所有的人都出席。

all 表示「一切」時用單數：

All is lost.　一切都失去了。

(3)指人的不定代名詞可以有's 所有格。例如：

no one's fault　沒有人的錯

everybody's duty　每個人的責任

⑷ all、both、every、each、some、any、either、neither、no 可以直接置於名詞前面，當定詞(determiner)使用。例如：

all students　所有的學生　　*both plans*　兩個計劃
every teacher　每個教師　　*each girl*　各個女孩子
some water　一些水　　　　*either parent*　父母中任一個

⑸ all、both 及 every 與否定詞 not 連用時，通常表示部分否定。例如：

1. a.*Every* man can *not* be a teacher.　並非人人都能當老師。
   b.*Not every* man can be a teacher.　並非人人都能當老師。
2. a.*All* of the boys are *not* hungry.　並非所有的男孩子們都餓了。
   b.*Not all* of the boys are hungry.　並非所有的男孩子們都餓了。
3. a.*Both* of them are *not* nervous.　他們兩人並非都是緊張的。
   b.*Not both* of them are nervous.　他們兩人並非都是緊張的。

注意：⑷上面三例句中 a、b 兩種說法都表示「部分否定」，但以 b 的說法比較明確。

⑸上面三例句的「全部否定」的說法分別是：

1. No man can be a teacher.　沒有人能當老師。
2. None of the boys are hungry.　這些男孩子全部都不餓。
3. Neither of them are nervous.　他們兩個人都不緊張。

(6) some(以及其複合詞如 someone、somebody、something)通常用於肯定句; any(以及其複合詞 anyone、anybody、anything)通常用於否定句、疑問句、及條件句。例如:

1. We have *some* money.　我們有一些錢。

2. Do you have *any* money?　你們有錢嗎?

　　Yes, we have *some*.　有，我們有一些。

　或 No, we don't have *any*.　沒有，我們沒有錢。

3. Don't let *anyone* in.　不要讓任何人進來。

4. If *anything* happens, call me at once.　如果有任何事情發生，立即打電話給我。

(7) one 可表示‘一個’(數目／量)，並代替名詞，避免重複，也可泛指所有的人。例如:

1. I have two donuts. Would you like *one*?　我有兩個甜甜圈。你要來一個嗎?

2. Do you have a pen?　你有筆嗎?

　　Yes, I do. I have *one*.（＝a pen）有的，我有一枝。

3. *One* should study hard.　人應該用功讀書。(泛指所有的人)

(8) no one 意思是「無一人」(只用來指人)，與單數動詞連用。none 表示「無一人，或物」(可指人或物)，在比較傳統的用法中，none 與單數動詞連用，但現在的用法常與複數動詞連用。

1. *No one* likes him.　沒有人喜歡他。

2. *None* are (is) happy with this result.　沒有人對這結果感到高興。

⑼ other 可加 s 成爲複數；another 只能有單數。例如：

　1. I don't like these shirts. Show me some *others.*　我不喜歡這些襯衣，拿一些別的給我看看。

　2. This hat is too big. Show me *another,* please.　這頂帽子太大了，請拿另外一頂給我看看。

⑽ either 與 neither 都只能指兩個人或事物，只與單數動詞連用。例如：

　1. *Either* of the brothers *is* at home now.　現在他兩兄弟中會有一人在家。

　2. *Neither* of them *is* happy.　他們兩人都不快樂。

⑾many 與 few 指可數名詞；much 與 little 指不可數名詞。例如：

　1. *Many* of the *students* have left.　學生當中很多人都已經走了。

　2. *Few* of *them* said good-bye to their teacher.　他們當中沒幾個人對他們的老師說再見。

　3. *Much* of his *money* has been wasted.　他的錢很多都浪費了。

　4. *Little* of the *truth* is known.　此事的眞相人們所知不多。

注意：few 與 little 含有**否定的語意**，因此 few 是「**很少**」(沒幾個)之意；little 是「**很少**」(沒多少)之意。表示「一些」、「幾個」、「少數」時，用 *a few*；表示「一點」、「少量」時，用 *a little*(如 a few of the books, a few books；a little of the milk, a little milk 等)。

13.5. 指示代名詞

　　指示代名詞(Demonstrative Pronouns)主要用來**指明特定的人或事物**。主要的指示代名詞為 this、these、that、those，另外，有些文法書認為 some、such 與 so 也屬於指示代名詞。除 this 與 that 有複數形式(these 與 those)以外，指示代名詞的格與數都沒有特別的字形。例如：

1. ***This*** is an air-conditioner.　這是一部冷氣機。

2. ***That*** is John's cap.　那是 John 的帽子。

3. ***These*** are new books. ***Those*** are old ones.　這些是新書。那些是舊書。

注意：⒜this 與 these 指比較接近說話者的人或事物。而 that 與 those 則指離說話者比較遠的人或事物。

　　⒝在社交場合中，介紹別人時可以用 this。例如：

1. Tom: John, ***this*** is Miss Wang.

　　Tom 對 John 說：「John，這是王小姐。」

　　⒞打電話時，說出打電話者自己身分時，可以用 this。例如：

2. 電話裏: Hello. ***This*** is Tom Wilson. Can I speak to Tony Wang, please?

　　電話裏：喂，我是 Tom Wilson。可以跟 Tony Wang 說話嗎？

　　⒟same、so、such 的用法對初學者而言比較複雜，我們不擬在本書中提出。有興趣的讀者可參看拙著《簡明現代英文法》第十四章，14.4.2. 至 14.4.4. 節。

13.6. 相互代名詞

(1) **相互代名詞**(Reciprocal Pronouns)有 each other 與 one another 兩種形式。例如:

 1. Tom and Mary helped *each other.* Tom 與 Mary 互相幫助。

 2. The students in that class can take care of *one another.* 那個班上的學生能夠互相照顧。

注意: 傳統文法強調兩者之間(如例句1)用 each other, 兩者以上(如例句2)則用 one another。但事實上很多情況下 each other 與 one another 是可以通用的。只是 each other 比較不正式, one another 比較正式而已。

(2) each other 與 one another 可以有所有格。例如:

The students borrowed *each other's* (或 *one another's*) notebook. 學生們互相借(對方的)筆記本。

(3) each other 與 one another 的先行詞必須是複數。例如:

 1. *Peter and Mary* trust *each other* (或 *one another*). Peter 與 Many 互相信任(對方)。

 2. *They* love *each other* (*one another*). 他們相愛。

(4) each other 及 one another 不可作句子的主詞。

13.7.　疑問代名詞

在第十章＜問句的形成＞中，我們討論過 wh-問句。在 wh-問句中作主詞、受詞或主詞補語使用的疑問詞 who、whom、whose、which、what 也稱為疑問代名詞(Interrogative Pronouns)。例如：

1. ***Who*** came here?　誰到這兒來?
2. ***Who*** ／ ***Whom*** did you see?　你看見了誰?
3. ***Whose*** is this?　這是誰的?
4. ***Which*** do you prefer?　你比較喜歡哪個?
5. ***What*** do you want?　你想要什麼?

注意：whom 為受格，但在當代英語中很少用。上面例句2用 who 比較自然。但是，在介詞後面則要用 whom。例如：With whom did you talk?(你跟誰說話?)。然而，這種說法是非常正式的說法，在口語中，通常說 Who did you talk with?

更多有關疑問代名詞的例句，參看第十章第 10.3.節。

13.8.　關係代名詞

關係代名詞(Relative Pronouns)**除了可以指稱其先行詞以外，還可以引導「關係子句」**。關係代名詞有 who、whom、whose、which、that 等。例如：

1. I know the boy ***who*** came to your store yesterday.　我認識那個昨天到你店裏的男孩子。

2. The boy *who* / *whom* you saw yesterday is my student.
你昨天看見的那個男孩子是我的學生。

3. The girl *whose* father is a lawyer is also my student.
父親當律師的那個女孩子也是我的學生。

4. I like the book *that* / *which* you bought yesterday.
我喜歡你昨天買的那本書。

5. The book *that* / *which* is on the desk is mine.　桌上的那本書是我的。

6. The book *whose* cover is green is John's.　封面是綠色的那本書是 John 的。

注意: who / whom 只指人, whose 可指人或物, that 可以指人或物, which 只能指物。

有關關係代名詞詳細的用法, 參看全書有討論「關係子句」的一章。

13.9. 不定代名詞、指示代名詞、疑問代名詞的形容詞用法

不定代名詞、指示代名詞、疑問代名詞中, 大多數都可以置於名詞前面, 當形容詞使用。例如:

1. *Any* student can answer that question.　任何學生都能回答這問題。

2. *Some* students are late.　有些學生遲到。

3. *Every* student has his own book.　每個學生都有自己的書。

4. *Both* students failed in the exam.　這兩個學生考試都不及格。

5. I want *another* pencil.　我要另外一枝鉛筆。

6. *Many* students don't like English.　很多學生不喜歡英文。

7. *Which* lesson do you like?　你喜歡哪一課?

8. *What* color do you like?　你喜歡什麼顏色?

9. *Whose* hat is this?　這是誰的帽子?

10. I like *this ／ that* pen.　我喜歡這／那枝筆。

11. *These ／ Those* students are very diligent. 這／那些學生很勤勉。

《習題 17》

(A)在下列各句中，使用正確的代名詞，並標明其文法功能。使用以下符號：

　S＝主詞, O＝受詞, SC＝主詞補語, OP＝介詞受詞

　例：Our teacher saw John and (I) _____.

　　　Our teacher saw John and *me*.(O)

1. Tom and (I) _____ have come.

2. A: Who is it?

　B: It's (I) _____.

3. She sent a letter to (he) _____.

4. (We) _____ students like holidays.

5. The book was given to (she) _____ and (I) _____.

6. The teacher is taking (they) _____ to the museum.

7. Mr. Wang saw (she) _____.

(B)填入適當的代名詞所有格形式。

　例：He borrowed (I) _____ book.

　　　He borrowed *my* book.

1. The dog is wagging (搖動) (it) _____ tail.

2. (Who) _____ book is this?

3. Every teacher has (he) _____ own teaching methods.

4. Tom didn't bring his pencil, so I let him use (I) _____ .

5. Can you tell me which room is (they) _____ ?

6. Here are some boxes. (Who) _____ are they? Are they(you) _____ ?

7. Mr. and Mrs. Lin told (they) _____ children to come home on Sunday.

8. Mary is on (she) _____ way to school.

(C)以獨立所有格(如 mine, yours, his 等)取代括號中的字。

　例： This book is (my book).

　　　 This book is *mine*.

1. I lost my watch. Can I borrow (your watch)?

2. This raincoat is (my raincoat).

3. I have my friends and you have (your friends).

4. She doesn't want my help; she wants (your help).

5. My guess (猜測) is as good as (your guess).

6. She has finished her homework, but I haven't finished (my homework).

7. This is my ticket. Where is (her ticket)?

8. Our plan is different from (his plan).

(D)填入適當的反身代名詞。

　例： Tom cut *himself*.

1. She bought _____ a dress.

2. Peter only thinks about _____ .

3. He wrote a story about ＿＿＿＿.

4. Did you enjoy ＿＿＿＿ at the party?

5. She hurt ＿＿＿＿.

6. Tom blamed (責怪) ＿＿＿＿ for being late.

7. I can see ＿＿＿＿ in the mirror.

(E)填入適當的泛稱用法代名詞。

例：*We* should obey *our* parents when *we* are young.

1. ＿＿＿＿ never know what will happen in the future.

2. ＿＿＿＿ all need rest and relaxation.

3. ＿＿＿＿ say it's going to rain tomorrow.

4. When ＿＿＿＿ are sick, ＿＿＿＿ need to see doctors.

5. ＿＿＿＿ should love ＿＿＿＿ country.

(F)把下列各句翻譯成英文。

1.今天很冷。

2.現在幾點鐘了?

3.現在是八點鐘。

4.從這兒到臺中有多遠?

5.這兒很黑。

(G)填入適當的動詞與代名詞。

例：Each of the boys *is* doing *his* own work.

　　All of the boys *are* doing *their* own work.

1. All the students ＿＿＿＿ (be) bringing ＿＿＿＿ own lunch boxes.

2. Each of the pencils ＿＿＿＿ (belong 屬於) to John.

3. Either of the men ＿＿＿＿ (be) happy.

4. Everyone will try to do_____ best.

5. Neither of the plan (計劃)_____ good.

6. Both of the students_____ (be) nervous.

7. All of us_____ (seem) to feel satisfied (滿意).

(H)填入 some 或 any。

1. Do you have_____money?

2. He bought_____new furniture yesterday.

3. The cat is hidden (躲藏起來) in_____place.

4. Do you have_____difficulty in doing your homework?

5. I don't know_____ of his friends.

6._____of my students were tired.

7. You can't answer_____of these questions.

8. If you have_____problem, we can help you with it.

(I)填入 little 或 few。

1. I have _____ interest in study mathematics.

2. _____people will help him.

3. She has learned very _____ about English grammar (文法).

4. The man told the boys to sit down, but _____ listened to him.

5. I have very _____ time for this.

6._____ of the students look happy.

第十四章
主詞與動詞的一致

14.1. 語詞的一致

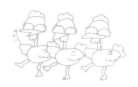

　　英語文法中, 有些語詞要配合使用, 稱為語詞的一致(agreement)。這種一致的現象主要有兩種。一種是代名詞與其指稱(先行詞)的一致, 例如 the man——he／him／his, the girl——she／her 等。另一種則是動詞與主詞的一致。例如 **The boy is** here, **The boys are** here。前者在第十三章〈代名詞〉已經討論過。本章只討論後者。

14.2. 主詞與動詞一致的一些原則

　　(1)主詞後面接片語修飾語時, 動詞通常與主詞一致, 片語中的名詞通常與動詞形式無關。例如:

　　1. A **box** of nails **is** on the table.　桌子上有一盒釘子。(真正主詞是 box 盒子)
　　2. Two **boxes** of candy **are** stolen.　兩盒糖果被偷了。

3. **Tom,** together with all his students, **has** just arrived here. Tom 和他所有的學生剛剛到達這裡。

(2)主詞含有兩個或兩個以上用 and 來連接起來的名詞時，動詞通常用複數。例如：

1. **Tom and Peter are** students. Tom 和 Peter 是學生。
2. **The pen and the paper are** on the desk. 筆和紙都在桌上。
3. **Brenda, Angela, and Dennis are** good friends.
   Brenda、Angela 和 Dennis 三人是好朋友。

但如用 and 連接起來的名詞指的是同一個人或同一事物或概念時，動詞用單數。例如：

1. **Curry and Chicken is** my favorite dish. 咖哩雞是我喜愛的一道菜。
2. **My old friend and colleague,** Harry, **has** just gone to New York. 我的老朋友也是同事 Harry 剛去了紐約。

(3)兩個或兩個以上的名詞由or，或either…or，或neither…nor，或not only…but (also)連接時，動詞與最接近動詞的名詞一致。例如：

1. Mr. Wang or **his children have** to do this job. 王先生或他的孩子們必須做這工作。
2. Either you or **he is** responsible for this. 你或是他要對此事負責。
3. Neither they nor **I was** mistaken. 他們和我都沒錯。
4. Not only the students, but (also) **the teacher is** going to help me. 不止學生們，連老師也會幫助我。

但注意：如兩個名詞由 *as well as* 連接時，動詞與前面的第一個名詞
　　一致。例如：

　5. *Nelson,* as well as you, *is* tired.　Nelson 和你都累了。

(比較：Not only you but also Nelson is tired.)

　⑷集合名詞(如 audience ‘觀衆’、committee ‘委員會’、family ‘家
庭’、class ‘班’、company ‘同伴、一群人’、group ‘一群’、assembly
‘大會’、government ‘政府’、jury ‘陪審團’ 等)被視作一個獨立單位
或組織時，動詞用單數；如表示該群體或集合中的個別成員的總和時，動詞
用複數。例如：

　1. My family *is* not very large.　我的家並不是大家庭。(指人口
　　不多)

　2. My family *are* all happy about this.　我全家人對此事都感
　　到很高興。

　3. The committee *is* going to hold its first meeting next
　　week.　委員會下週舉行第一次會議。

　4. The committee *have disagreed* among themselves.　委員
　　會中的委員們意見不一致。

　⑸以下的不定代名詞通常與單數動詞連用：each、everybody、every-
one、everything、any、anybody、anyone、anything、somebody、
someone、something、one、no one、nothing、none、nobody、either、
neither、another、the other。例如：

　1. *Everything is* O.K.　一切都好。

　2. *No one is* perfect.　沒有人是完美的。

　3. *Someone wants* to see you.　有人想見你。

4. **Something is** missing.　缺少了一些東西。

5. **None** has come on time.　沒有人準時到。

注意：none 也可以與複數動詞連用。例如：None have come on time.

(6)以下不定代名詞(以及其形容詞的用法)指人時通常與複數動詞連用：all、both、a few、few、many、several、some。例如：

1. **All** are here.　所有的人都在這兒。

2. **Several have** come.　有幾個人來了。

3. **Several students are** absent.　有幾個學生缺席。

4. **Both are** happy.　兩個人都快樂。

注意：(a) all 指事物或情況時, 動詞用單數。例如：**All is** quiet here. 這裡一切平靜。

(b)「Many a＋名詞」與單數動詞連用。例如：**Many a man wants** to have a better education.　很多人想受更好的教育。

(7)主詞是「A number of＋名詞」時, 動詞用複數(因為 a number of＝several, 為複數語意的修飾語)；主詞是「The number of＋名詞」時, 動詞用單數(因為真正的主詞是 the number, of＋名詞只是修飾語)。例如：

1. **A number of students** in my class **are** very lazy.　我班上有幾個學生十分懶惰。

2. **The number** of students in my class **is** too large.　我班上學生的數目太大了(學生太多了)。

3. **The number** of students in the composition class **is lim-**

ited to 10.　作文課班上學生的數目限定爲 10 個。

(8) A lot of、lots of、plenty of 等表示「多量、大量」語意的片語所引導的主詞, 亦即「a lot of 等＋名詞」, 其數通常取決於 of 之後的名詞。例如:

1. *A lot of people have* gathered around the gate. 很多人已聚集在門口。
2. *A lot of money was* given to the poor people.　很多錢送給了窮人。

另外, 下列片語亦很常用:

(a) a good many (of)、a great many (of) '很多、許多' ［等於 many, 與複數名詞及動詞連用］
(b) a good deal (of)、a great deal (of) '很多、大量' ［等於 much, 與不可數名詞及單數動詞連用］

(9) 表示「部分」及「分數」語詞 (partitives) 如 half of '一半'、one third of '三分之一'、one fourth of '四分之一'、part of '部分' 等所引導的主詞, 其數常取決於這些「表部分語詞」後面的名詞。如名詞爲單數, 動詞用單數, 如名詞爲複數, 動詞則用複數。例如:

1. *Half of* the *boys are* here.　男孩子們有半數在這兒。
2. *Half of* the *crude oil is* imported.　有一半原油是進口的。
3. *Twenty percent* of the *people live* in this part of the city.　百分之二十的人住在城市的這一區。
4. *Thirty percent* of our drinking *water comes* from that lake.　我們的飲用水有百分之三十取自那個湖。
5. *Part of* the *money was* stolen.　部分的錢被偷走了。
6. *One fourth of* the students *were* absent.　四分之一的學生

缺席。

7. *One fourth of* our *time is* wasted. 我們的時間有四分之一浪費掉。

⑽表示時間、重量、距離、價格等語詞如看作一個總數時，動詞用單數。例如：

1. Two hundred miles *is* a long distance. 兩百哩是一段長距離。

2. Two million dollars *is* a large sum of money. 兩百萬元是數目很大的一筆錢。

3. Thirty days *seems* to be a long time. 三十天似乎是一段長時間。

但是，如果表示這些數目中個別的成分時，用複數。例如：

4. There *are thirty days* in a month. 一個月有三十天。

5. *Three thousand dollars have* been spent on the project. 三千元已經花在那個計劃上了。

⑾導詞主詞 it 與單數動詞連用。例如：

1. *It is* wrong to tell lies. 說謊是不對的。

2. *It is* true that she is John's cousin. 她真的是 John 的表姊。

⑿There 作引導的句子，亦即 there 作前導主詞時，動詞取決於真正的主詞。(通常 there 為「虛詞」，並無語意，真正的主詞是「There＋be＋名詞」中，be 動詞後面的名詞。例如：

1. There *is* a *pencil* on the desk. 桌上有一枝鉛筆。

2. There **are** thousands of **books** in the library.　圖書館中有
上千本書。

《習題 18》

(A)填入正確的 be 動詞(用過去式)。

　　例：_All_ of his _students were_ here.

　　　　All of the _milk was_ sour.

1. Most of his money＿＿＿＿stolen.

2. Most of his books＿＿＿＿stolen.

3. None of the cakes ＿＿＿＿eaten.

4. All of the fruit ＿＿＿＿eaten.

5. All of the apples ＿＿＿＿eaten.

6. Half of the students ＿＿＿＿gone.

7. Half of the roast beef (烤牛肉)＿＿＿＿eaten.

8. Some of the boys ＿＿＿＿very helpful.

9. Some of the information (資訊)＿＿＿＿very helpful.

(B)在下列各句中，以括號把主詞標出，並在與動詞一致的字底下劃線，再在空格中填
入正確的動詞形式。動詞提示於句後。用現在時式。

　　例：(The _boys_ in my class) _are_ happy. (be)

1. The police ＿＿＿＿ working on this case now. (be)

2. Our football team ＿＿＿＿ the best one in the country. (be)

3. No frozen meat (冷凍肉) ＿＿＿＿sold here. (be)

4. The crew (全體船員) ＿＿＿＿getting sick. (be)

5. A knowledge of English grammar ＿＿＿＿very helpful. (be)

6. A little learning _____ a dangerous thing. (be)

7. A number of students _____ to bring their lunch boxes. (forget)

8. The number of people who want to help us _____ small. (be)

(C)選擇正確的形式。

1. Each of these T-shirts (is, are) green.

2. One of her best friends (wants, want) to help us.

3. Everyone in both classes (was, were) excited.

4. Tom, as well as his parents, (was, were) happy about my decision.

5. Some of your answers (was, were) wrong.

6. Everyone in this country (pays, pay) an annual income tax(所得稅).

7. One of her sisters (is, are) leaning French.

8. English (has, have) always been my favorite subject.

9. The news (is, are) very interesting.

10. Two thousand dollars (is, are) all we need.

11. Darts (is, are) his favorite game.

12. Ten minutes (is, are) enough for me to finish this exercise.

13. There (is, are) several ways in answering this question.

14. Not only you but also I (are, am) mistaken.

15.(Has, Have) all the tickets been sold?

16. Tom, together with his three brothers, (is, are) leaving for Hong Kong tomorrow.

17. That (is, are) very interesting.

(D)使用正確的動詞形式，用現在時式。

　例：Either John or his wife _has_ said that. (have)

1. Many a junior high school student (國中學生) never _____ to study

English. (like)

2. Three fourths of the money_____already been spent. (have)

3. Twenty-five percent of our students_____lazy. (be)

4. The family _____agreed among themselves to move to the new house next week. (have)

5. The members of the committee _____reached an agreement. (have)

6. Everyone of my students _____the joke. (know)

7. Neither the doctor nor the nurse _____responsible for the accident. (be)